NICK'S DESTINY

GHOST ORACLE BOOK 6

ROGER HYTTINEN

RAMBLING WORDSMITH PRESS

I wish to thank you for reading my work. Please consider leaving a review wherever you purchased this book. Also, consider telling your friends about it to help me spread the word about my book.

Visit:

rogerhyttinen.com

CHECK OUT MY OTHER BOOKS

<u>Standalones</u>

A Touch of Cedar

Christmas Cookies that Sparkle

Pushed Under the Mistletoe

<u>Ghost Oracle Series:</u>

Nick's Awakening (Ghost Oracle Book 1)

Anaconda! (Ghost Oracle Book 2)

The Magician's Secret (Ghost Oracle Book 3)

Ghost at the Prom (Book 4)

Camping with A Ghost (Book 5)

<u>Wolves of Norbury series:</u>

Norian's Gamble

JOIN MY NEWSLETTER

Want to know be the first to know when I release a new book?

Then join my newsletter.

Be the first to know when I have a new book coming out and get plenty of freebies and other goodies, too (like a free short story in your inbox every Monday!).

Enter the following URL in your browser: https://roger-hyttinen.com/newsletter

CHAPTER ONE

THE GALLOWSPINE MOUNTAINS ROSE UP FROM THE horizon like hundreds of dark fingers reaching for the heavens. The sky was a deep purple, with wisps of gray clouds drifting across its surface. A few stars had appeared in the sky; without the sun to obscure them, their light was strong and steady. Mist clung to their jagged peaks and ridges, shrouding the mountains in mystery.

A convoy of vehicles moved slowly along the winding mountain road. An eclectic group of psychics from various countries throughout the world sat inside their armored trucks and SUVs as they wound through the deep green forest. Within these vehicles, they all had a common goal: to travel to Gallowspine Mountains and take part in a war — a war against them and everything they stood for.

Nick stood outside the resort, his feet frozen to the spot. He locked his eyes on the winding road leading up to the grand gates, watching anxiously as headlights sliced through the night's darkness. With each minute that passed, his heart grew heavier with anticipation and dread. The icy wind carried with it a chill that penetrated to all his bones, but nothing could compare to the chill of uncertainty that crawled across his skin.

He'd spent days preparing for this very moment, scrubbing every corner of the vast vacation resort until it shone like new. He opened all the windows to let in fresh air, arranged the furniture into its rightful place, and filled the kitchen cupboards with enough food to last weeks. But no amount of preparation could quell the questions swimming in his mind. Questions to which he was desperately seeking answers.

Nick watched as the cars wound their way up the driveway to the resort. His heart raced in anticipation and sweat formed on his palms. As the first car pulled around the corner, he could make out two figures inside — an elderly woman and a young man, both dressed in brightly colored clothes. He felt a shiver of excitement run through him as they emerged from the vehicle.

The other cars followed suit, each disgorging several more men and women. They all had a certain air of authority, like royalty. Nick felt himself trembling as he watched them alight from their vehicles, laughing and smiling, seemingly unaware of his presence.

Nick stepped forward, his body trembling in the glow of the resort. He bowed deeply and spoke with a shaky voice, "Welcome! It's an honor to meet all of you." The visitors seemed taken aback by his sudden appearance but still managed to crack grins, exchanging friendly banter with Nick. The last man to exit the vehicle was Nate, his late uncle's friend and fellow psychic. Nick recognized him immediately as they had video conferenced several times.

Nate stepped forward and embraced Nick warmly as the others watched on in silence. "My dear boy," he said softly, "It's so good to finally see you in person." His words were heavy with emotion as he released Nick from his embrace. "My goodness, you look just like your Uncle Mitch when he was young."

The rest of the group stood in awkward silence as they watched this reunion unfold before them. After what felt like an eternity, Nate finally turned to them and said, "This is my dear friend Nick Michelson — the one we've all been talking about for months on end."

Nick could feel himself blushing as he stood there motionless before them all. He stepped away from Nate and took a deep breath before introducing himself formally to the group. He spoke with confidence and a steady voice — something that hadn't always come so easily for him — as he welcomed everyone and thanked them for coming so far to join this important mission.

There were smiles all around at this gesture of hospitality; it seemed like it was finally enough to break the ice between them all. They began talking amongst themselves about what they expected from this trip and how each of their individual skills would help them succeed in their quest ahead.

Nick listened intently as each person shared their stories, feeling an overwhelming sense of pride wash over him at being part of such a gifted group of people.

"Let me show you where you'll be staying," Nick said. He gestured for the group to follow him through a large wooden door. He stepped into the grand hall first, and everyone gasped at its magnificence. The walls were made of beige stone, as were the floors that held the weight of their footsteps as they looked up at the towering ceiling. Elaborately carved furniture filled the room, flanked by luxuriously heavy purple curtains. In front of them was a wide staircase that curved gracefully upward, dotted with potted plants full of white and purple flowers. A soft breeze billowed through the open door. Everyone stood in awe at the bottom of the steps as their shoes clicked against its surface in a gentle echo.

Nick pointed up the stairs. "There's a bunch of rooms up there. You can choose whatever ones you like."

With that, the visitors began dragging their luggage up the staircase while Nate disappeared around a corner toward another room.

Nick's confidante and friend Katrina, who had been already waiting inside the resort, hurried to his side, her face lined with worry. She spoke quietly, almost an eager whisper. "Nick, I think something's wrong," she said, glancing around fearfully. The warm light of candles flickered across her face as she continued. "Ever since we began preparing for their arrival, the spirits have grown increasingly restless. I can't shake the feeling that their energy is... growing stronger. Though I can't see them like you unless you're next to me, I can feel it in my gut."

Nick nodded. "Yeah, I've noticed it too. And there's one spirit in particular." He closed his eyes and murmured, "Show yourself," under his breath before opening them again to see a figure manifesting beside him. It was foggy in form and barely visible against the dim light of the room, but Katrina could make out its features — an old man with a gray beard wearing a tattered suit. She gasped at the sudden apparition.

The ghost spoke in a hollow, mournful voice and looked at Nick with sorrowful eyes. "Nicholas," he said, "You must listen to me. It is of the utmost importance that I protect you."

Nick felt a chill run through him. "Protect me from what?"

The ghost shimmered and faded out of existence, only to reappear a moment later. He raised an ethereal hand to his brow solemnly, as if he had unlocked the answer to some mystery. His voice echoed when he spoke: "That is not for you to know... yet," he said, looking at Katrina with piercing eyes that seemed to glow from within. Nick and Katrina exchanged an uneasy glance and watched as the specter slowly faded away without another word, leaving them stunned by the strange encounter.

Nick spoke first, breaking the silence. "What in the hell was that?"

"I have no idea," Katrina replied, her voice trembling with confusion.

"Did you hear what he said?"

Katrina nodded, still shaken by the experience. "Let's just get out of here before he comes back. He gave me the creeps."

But before they could move, Nate's silhouette emerged from the large dining room. As he neared, his stern face became clear, eyes filled with a mix of concern and determination. "Nick, were you just talking to...."

"A ghost. Yeah, yeah, I know. I'm not supposed to be helping spirits." He paused and cleared his throat before continuing in a softer tone of voice. "But I didn't have any say in the matter. He just..."

"It's true," Katrina cut in. "He just appeared in front of us and started saying how he had to protect Nick."

Nate's wrinkled brow deepened as he considered this new information. "Protect you? Did he say from whom or what?"

Nick shook his head. "Nope. I asked him the same question. But he wouldn't tell me."

"Hmm...most curious," said Nate. "Did he threaten you?"

"No, the opposite, actually. He said he wanted to help me. Or something to that effect."

"Listen, gentlemen, I'm going to pop into the other room with the others," Katrina said. "I'll let you two catch up."

Nick tilted his head and watched her walk away. He turned to Nate, who was watching him with an expression of curiosity. "I want to ask you something."

After Nate nodded once, Nick lifted one hand to make a wide sweeping gesture with both hands. "Why here? Why not just meet in Europe?"

Nate furrowed his brow. "Pardon?"

"Here in Gallowspine Mountains, I mean," Nick said, his voice tense with a mixture of curiosity and apprehension. "Of all places in the world, why did you and the other psychics come here?"

Nate sighed deeply. "Ah. Well, there are two reasons. First, we know Leo, the shadow demon, is here because of you. As we all know, he's got a vendetta against psychic mediums, and you, my boy, are particularly in his crosshairs." He paused, letting the gravity of the statement sink in. "Second, Gallowspine isn't just another mountain range. It's the most haunted place in the world, even more haunted than Edinburgh. There's ancient power here, Nick — power we can use to our advantage."

Nick swallowed hard, memories of his last encounter with Leo flooding back. The demonic face, the malevolent aura, and the sheer terror he'd felt. "It's such an odd coincidence that my family moved here, of all places."

Nate leaned against the wall, his gaze distant. "Sometimes, Nick, it's not about choices. With your extraordinary abilities, there's a good chance Gallowspine chose your family and not the other way around. Perhaps because of this very battle that's unfolding."

Feeling the weight of the revelations, Nick slumped down into a nearby chair. "So what's next?"

Nate stepped beside him, placing a reassuring hand on Nick's shoulder. "Tonight we rest, tomorrow, we convene. The psychics have some crucial information they want to share with you. We're thinking brunch, catered, to keep everyone comfortable, something low-key. Can you take care of that?"

Nick nodded slowly, then hesitated. "My family... they need to be safe."

"I agree," Nate said firmly. "They should stay with us at the resort. All of us together can offer them protection."

But later that night, convincing his family proved much more difficult than Nick had imagined. The dimly lit living room became a stage for the conflict, an arena for the battle of wills in which his vision for them clashed with their refusal to leave their home. Nick, desperate to ensure his family's safety, pleaded, "Mom and Dad, you have to trust me. You need to stay at the resort with the others."

His father's face remained resolute. "This is our home, Nick. We've faced challenges before."

Nick's frustration grew, but he also knew revealing everything would jeopardize his younger sister's innocence. She sat obliviously upstairs in her room, unaware of the dark forces threatening her world.

"You don't understand. Leo could show up at any moment! He might come for you!" Nick said, fighting back tears.

His father nodded with a small smile. "You have always been brave. And so are we. We will stand strong together, just like we always do. We're a formidable family, son. If trouble comes, we will meet it head on."

His mother, sensing his genuine fear, hugged him. "We'll be vigilant, Nick. You've always protected us. And remember how you chased Leo away last time?"

Nick bit his lip, the memories vivid. "I was lucky then. I don't know if I can be that fortunate again."

At that, Missy, his little sister, marched into the room full of indignation. Nick wondered how long she'd been eavesdropping. She shot a glance at her brother. "What are you all talking about? Why won't you tell me what's going on? And who's Leo? And why did Nick chase him away?" She crossed her arms over her chest.

Nick's mother let out an exasperated sigh. "Not now Melissa. Go back up to your room until we're done talking. I'll come up afterwards." As she heard her mother's last words, Missy charged out of the room with a huff and stomped up the stairs, her feet hammering on each riser. She slammed the door to her room so hard that the windows rattled in their frame.

"I swear, that girl," Nick's mother said.

"Maybe it's time to tell her," Nick suggested quietly, turning towards his mother.

She shook her head resolutely. "No, not yet. Maybe when this is all over. I don't want to scare her with everything that's going on right now. Let her keep her innocence for a little while longer."

CHAPTER TWO

Hidden among the dense trees of the woods, stood a small cabin that Nick had inherited from his late Uncle Mitch. It was Nick and Gabe's private weekend retreat, a place where they'd share moments away from the world — a place where they shared their hearts and their bodies. Today, however, the fury of the outside wind and the rustling of the leaves served as a haunting backdrop to a grave conversation.

Inside, the cabin was cozy with rustic charm. A rich, earthy scent of wood and spices permeated the air. Smooth wooden beams crisscrossed the ceiling, and a fireplace took center stage, the flames casting flickering shadows on the walls. But despite the fire's warmth, there was a chill in the air. Tonight, the atmosphere inside was thick with tension.

Gabe, pouring a cup of tea, looked over at Nick, who paced the length of the cabin, his footsteps echoing softly against the hardwood floor. The crackling fire in the cabin's hearth cast a warm glow, contrasting the icy dread that gripped Nick's heart. He pursed his lips with concern, his eyes darting about as he thought through what needed to be done next. Another crackle erupted from the fireplace, startling him.

Gabe set aside the teapot with a loud clink.

"You've been acting super weird ever since we got here, Nick," Gabe remarked, his voice laced with worry. "Are you going to tell me what's up or what?"

The wind howled through the cracks of the cabin's aged wooden walls. Nick shivered as the icy blast found its way through. Flickering firelight cast dim shadows on Gabe's concerned face, making his bright blue eyes look haunted. The lines of worry etched into his boyfriend's brow deepened by the mounting threat of Leo, the shadow demon.

Nick slowly turned to face Gabe with a heavy sigh. With determination in his eyes, he declared, "There's no easy way to say this, but I need you to leave, Gabe. Get as far away from Gallowspine Mountains as you can."

Gabe staggered back in shock. "W-why? What are you talking about?"

Nick stepped forward and took Gabe's hands in his own. He knew how difficult this conversation would be, but he had to make Gabe understand. He made a sweeping gesture with his arm. "You know why. Leo is out there somewhere, and he might come after you just to get to me." His grip tightened around Gabe's fingers as he pleaded, desperation in his eyes. "Please, Gabe, get away from Gallowspine Mountains before it's too late. I mean it."

Gabe groaned, his fingers running through his golden hair in frustration. "Nick, I'm scared as well," he said, "but I can't just take off from here. What would my mom and dad say? How could I explain it to them? I can't simply tell them that ghosts and demons are after me; they'd never believe it. If I told them I had to scramble out of town because an evil spirit was trying to hunt down me and Nick, and a bunch of psychics were going into battle against this demon, why — they'd have me locked up. You know this. You know how they are."

Nick's vision grew blurry as his eyes brimmed with tears. He desperately wanted Gabe to stay safe, no matter what happened to him. Still, he knew that this entire situation could lead to a dangerous end for both of them. His voice quivered as he spoke. "I can't risk you getting hurt for me. No matter what happens, I'll never forgive myself if something happened to you."

"I get that. But what is it you'd have me do? If I just up and left town by myself, my folks would call the police and launch a full-blown search for me. You know how over-protective they are."

"Isn't there any way you can convince them to go on a trip or something?" Nick asked and resumed pacing back and forth across the room. Back and forth he went, like a cat in a cage, always making sure he had a clear view of the window and the woods beyond it. He stopped in front of Gabe, his hands on his hips. "I just want you as far away from Gallowspine Mountains as possible when all this goes down."

"Look, I'll figure something out, okay?" Gabe replied, rubbing his temples. "It's hard enough dealing with the reality of Leo and the upcoming battle without trying to come up with a convincing lie for my parents as to why I need to suddenly leave town."

"Oh, I forgot to tell you," Nick blurted out, suddenly changing the subject. "The psychics arrived in town today. I'd rented a large, secluded chalet up the mountain where they'll be staying. They wanted to stay somewhere far away from town and away from people. I suppose in case Leo takes the battle to them."

"You mean the old ski resort up in the mountains?"

Nick nodded. "The owner was thrilled to have us there and said he welcomed the extra business. Though the resort was closed for the season, he was willing to open it up for us, which was nice of him. He knows my dad so I guess he made an exception for our stay. I had to clean it though because he'd already left for Phoenix for the winter. The caretaker let me in so I dusted, vacuumed up the cobwebs, and aired the place out before they all arrived. Most of the furniture was still covered in sheets. It kind of made me wonder what's the purpose of a caretaker is if they can't even do a little light dusting?"

Gabe raised an eyebrow, intrigued. "Your psychic friends — do you think they can actually stop Leo?"

"I don't know yet," Nick admitted, biting his lip. "We're all meeting tomorrow at the lodge so hopefully I'll learn more then. But at least I won't be alone in this fight."

A long moment of silence stretched out before them. "God, Nick, I'm so scared," Gabe whispered, the weight of his fear finally breaking through his carefully constructed facade. "What if we lose? What if Leo takes over everything?" He swallowed. "What if I lose you?"

"Hey," Nick said softly, pulling Gabe into his arms. He planted a soft kiss on Gabe's neck. "We're not gonna let any of that happen. We'll take Leo down with everything we have. Between me and the psychics, Leo doesn't stand a chance. I have faith in us. And just like my dad always says, 'failure is not an option.'"

Gabe straightened his shoulders and took a deep breath. "I hope you're right." His face was an inch from Nick's chest, and he made no move to pull back.

Nick laid a hand on Gabe's hip, pulled him closer, and felt the steady thump-thump of Gabe's heart beneath his palm, which matched his own heartbeat. "Of course I am," Nick murmured, his breath warm on the top of Gabe's head. However, as he spoke the words, a nagging doubt gnawed at him. Would he truly be able to stand by and watch the love of his life in danger if it came down to it? Never.

As they stood there, wrapped in each other's arms, the wind continued to howl outside. "As promised, I shall do the dishes," Gabe said. "It should only take a sec." With that, he broke their embrace and walked to the sink on the opposite wall. He grabbed the tan plastic dish pan and filled it up with hot water from the tap.

The fire in the cabin's hearth snapped and crackled, throwing outbreaks of radiant light onto the walls. Nick sat on the edge of the couch, his eyes following Gabe's every movement.

"Wait!" Gabe suddenly stopped, a spark of realization igniting in his eyes. He set down the cup he was holding near the basin. "Dude, I've got it! My grandma — she's been sick for a while now, remember?"

"Yeah, I remember," Nick replied. "But what does that have to do with getting you away from here?"

Gabe's eyes twinkled with excitement as he shared his plan. "Listen," he began, "I can tell my parents I want to go visit her alone. They know how much she means to me, and they'd never deny my request to see her one last time. Heck, maybe they'll even want to come with me." A small, hopeful smile curved his lips as he spoke.

But Nick's face creased in concern. He drew in his eyebrows in a worried frown. "Do you think they'd come with you?" he asked cautiously. "I'd be worried and would feel better if you weren't traveling alone right now." The words came out carefully as Nick tried not to let the doubt and worry for his boyfriend's safety and well-being show in his voice.

"I dunno, but if not, I'll be careful," Gabe reassured him. He took a deep breath and squeezed Nick's shoulder. "I promise. Besides, if I'm away from here, I won't be in the direct path of whatever Leo has in store. Just to be clear, I'm not a fan of leaving you to face that thing alone, but I know you're right. As much as it pains me to admit it, I don't want you to have to worry about protecting me, given that I have no psychic or witchy powers."

Nick acquiesced and stood up to wrap his arms around Gabe, the warmth of his embrace offering a momentary solace. He held Gabe tightly against his chest, trying to imprint the memory of this moment into his mind so he could hold on to it during the long nights ahead. "Alright," he whispered, his breath hot against Gabe's ear. "Just promise me you'll stay safe out there."

"I will," Gabe whispered into Nick's shoulder, momentarily overcome by the gravity of their situation. "But you're the one who needs to stay safe, mister."

As they stood there, embracing in the dim light, the fear and stress of the past few days seemed to melt away, leaving only pure emotion in its wake. Gabe pulled back slightly, gazing deeply into Nick's eyes before leaning in for a slow, tender kiss.

Their lips met, and the world outside ceased to exist. All that mattered now was the love they shared and the comfort they found in each other. As the kiss deepened, Nick felt a sudden surge of desire course through him — a need to be closer, to feel Gabe's skin against his own.

"Gabe," he murmured, pulling away just enough to speak, "I need you."

Gabe's breath caught in his throat as Nick's lips met his

own. "I need you too," he whispered, finally breaking the silence between them. "More than anything."

Nick led Gabe into the dimly lit bedroom. His heart pounded in his chest as he closed the door behind them, the sound of it slamming shut echoing through the quiet room.

Gabe's eyes met his, filled with desire and longing. He leaned in, capturing Gabe's lips in a deep, passionate kiss. Their bodies pressed together, skin on skin, as they explored each other with hungry hands. The scent of their combined cologne filled the air as they breathed heavily into each other's mouths.

The bed creaked softly beneath them as they sank deeper into their embrace, their limbs tangling together like vines. The room grew hazy around them as they lost themselves in the moment. Their hands roamed over each other's bodies, tracing every curve and line with reverent fingers. They spoke without words, their touch telling a story that only they could understand.

As they continued to explore each other's bodies with hungry lips and eager hands, time seemed to stand still. They were untouchable in this moment — invulnerable to the outside world and its troubles. And for a brief moment, all that mattered was the way their hearts beat in sync and the way their breaths mingled together in the quiet darkness of the room.

As the evening wore on, the two lost themselves in each other until finally exhaustion overcame them both and they fell deeply asleep in each other's arms.

CHAPTER THREE

NICK SAT AT THE LONG DINING ROOM TABLE, surrounded by his parents, his mentor Katrina, and the psychics who had come to Gallowspine Mountains to stand by his side. The smell of freshly brewed coffee filled the air as they waited for their post-brunch cuppa.

Nick's mother, the quintessential hostess, began with exaggerated politeness, "It's such an honor to meet all of you. We've heard so much about your talents."

Helena nodded, her gaze intense. "Thank you Mrs. Michelson but the time for pleasantries is short. There's a prophecy we must discuss." Helena gestured toward another woman, who nodded.

"Her people skills aren't the greatest, are they?" Katrina whispered into Nick's ear. He had to suppress a giggle.

The room went still, the only sound being the distant clatter of dishes.

Madam Celeste, a regal woman with silver hair and piercing blue eyes that seemed to see straight through Nick, began by stating, "We have gathered here today because a prophecy has been revealed, one that concerns you directly.

A powerful and reputable psychic foretold that the time will come when the Dark One, who we believe is the entity known as Leo, will rise and cause the dead to become powerful — more powerful than the living. Unfortunately, she has since passed on, but luckily for us, she documented her predictions in great detail, allowing us to study and learn from them. Thus far, everything she has predicted has come to pass, including an unknown entity who shall rise and snatch souls before they can cross over. Another predicted the murder of psychics by this same dark entity."

Nick shifted uncomfortably in his chair and took a sip of his coffee. His hands tightened around the edges of his napkin, crumpling it in his grip. He felt a sudden weight on his chest. His parents exchanged worried glances, while Katrina reached out to rest her hand on his arm, offering silent support.

An ominous chill crept through the air. "The prophecy speaks of a time when the Dark One will rise, an entity of unspeakable darkness and power who will grant the dead strength that eclipses that of the living. The Dark One, if left unchecked, will plunge our world into an age of despair." Her voice was low but firm, her gaze never leaving his as she continued. "The Light One, who we believe to be you, Nick, will also emerge, the only entity with the potential to halt the Dark One's reign." She paused for a moment to let the gravity of the situation sink in. "That is why we are all here. We must ensure that the Light One prevails."

Another psychic, a tall man named Raphael, added, "Should the Dark One prevail, the dead will hold more sway than the living. Spirits, once benign or indifferent, will become malevolent under the Dark One's thrall. The line between life and death will blur."

Katrina, her demeanor always calm and collected,

inquired, "Do you believe that this battle between light and dark is imminent?"

Helena nodded gravely, "We believe so. And if the Dark One prevails, we believe he plans to seize the Earth and possibly obliterate the Other Side, extinguishing its light, so souls find no solace. This is only speculation, mind you. But from what we gleamed from the prophecy and from readings, his intentions are not benevolent."

Nick's father, a practical man who was one to seek solutions rather than sit idle as a victim of fate, leaned forward in his chair and slid his hands together, fingertips touching beneath his chin as he peered at Helena over his thumbs. "But why gather here? Why now?"

For a moment, Nick thought he heard singing. The notes drifted on the air like leaves in a soft spring wind, swirling around him before fading away into silence. Nick cocked his head and looked around the room for the source. He glanced at the others, but nobody else at the table seemed to have heard what he did.

A younger psychic named Jasper responded to the question Nick's father had posed. "Because this is where it begins. The Gallowspine Mountains are a nexus of spiritual energy. And we are here to ensure that the Light One triumphs, no matter what."

Nick took a deep breath as he prepared to ask the question that gnawed at his insides. "I have a question," he said, his voice quavering and quiet. A hush swept over the room, and every head turned to look at him; every pair of eyes was fixed on him. "Why? Why me, I mean?"

Nick's mother, her voice trembling, interjected loudly, "Yes, why Nick? He's just a boy. He has no special powers, no armies, nothing. And he's only seventeen! Are you certain he's this... this Light One you speak of? How is my son supposed to defeat this ultimate evil?"

"Mrs. Michelson, the universe works in ways we can't always understand," Helena said. "Often, our strengths lie hidden, waiting for the right moment to manifest."

"And as for age, it's but a number, as they say," Madam Celeste said. "Nick's spirit, his essence, is ancient and powerful. His ability to see and interact with spirits, even at this young age, is testament to his unique role."

"Your abilities, your connection to the Other Side, it all points to you being the one chosen to face Leo," explained a younger psychic named Jasper, his voice tinged with both awe and fear. "The prophecy states that the Light One would have the power of visions and that your light will draw the dead to you. Based on everything Katrina and Nate have told us, it all points to you, Nick — of that, we have little doubt. You have the potential to save countless lives. But you must be prepared for the challenges ahead." Each of the psychics nodded in agreement, their stoic gaze affirming her words.

Helena added, "And that's why we are here. To guide Nick, to help him tap into his latent abilities, and to stand by his side. He might be young, but age is just a vessel. It's the spirit within that holds the power."

Helena added, "Nick is undoubtedly the Light One. It's not merely about his abilities, but also his resilience and courage. But he will not stand alone in this battle."

Raphael elaborated, "All of us, with our combined strength and knowledge, we will prepare Nick. We'll train him to harness his power, to amplify it, and to channel it against the Dark One."

Nick's mother hesitated, then said, "But he's never shown any signs of having... powers. How can you be so sure? I'm still not convinced. I'm not ready to send a young boy into a deadly battle without knowing for sure that he is the one you all think he is."

Maya added, "Throughout the annals of our history, there have been specific signs that distinguish the Light One. They're subtle, often manifesting in ways that might seem ordinary, but to trained eyes, they're unmistakable."

Nick, curiosity piqued, asked, "What are these signs?"

Raphael, with a small mysterious smile, replied, "First, the Light One is always born at the confluence of two celestial events, a lunar eclipse and a comet passing close to Earth. Nick, your birth coincided with this very phenomenon."

Helena continued, "Second, the Light One exhibits an innate connection with the spiritual realm. Your ability as a medium, especially at such a young age, is unparalleled. Such a connection to the spiritual realm is rare and potent. Nate has mentioned that Nick experiences visions, glimpses of the past and future. That alone is a tremendous advantage."

Helena interjected, "Imagine if we can harness that, anticipate the Dark One's moves, understand his past to find weaknesses. The battle isn't just about brute force; it's about strategy, understanding, and unity."

Maya gently approached Nick, "There's also a physical mark, often appearing in times of great stress or danger." She walked to where Nick was sitting. She reached out and gently turned Nick's wrist, revealing a faint but intricate pattern, like luminous veins of light, glowing subtly. "This mark," she whispered, "is the emblem of the Light One. Not just a birthmark, but a sign of destiny."

Nick's eyes widened in realization. "I always thought it was just a scar from when I fell as a child."

Raphael chuckled softly, "Fate has a way of weaving its design into the very fabric of our being, often disguising its grand design in the threads of everyday life."

Nick's mother, still processing everything, uttered, "So, all these signs... they all point to Nick?"

Helena nodded, "Yes. Each sign on its own could be dismissed as coincidence, but their confluence in your son is irrefutable. He is the Light One, destined to stand against the shadows."

Raphael, with a thoughtful expression, responded, "Throughout history, there have been other Light Ones. Each unique, each with their own set of talents tailored for their time and the challenges they faced. Not all powers manifest in ways that are obvious."

Nick's breathing quickened as the fear took over his body. Questions of how he could possibly prepare for such an unimaginable situation overwhelmed his mind. How could a mere mortal like himself — a high school student — ever hope to stand in the face of such darkness? His mind raced with images of dark powers and unearthly entities, and the thought of confronting them was enough to make his stomach clench in dread.

"Yes," Madam Celeste agreed, her gaze unwavering from Nick. "We will teach you everything we can in the short time we have, helping you to harness your powers and become the Light One you are destined to be."

Nick felt the weight of their expectations upon him, but deep down, he knew they were right. He knew what had to be done — he had to face Leo and protect the world from the darkness that threatened it. With a determined nod, he agreed to accept their help, embarking on a journey that would forever change the course of his life.

Katrina, after a moment of contemplation, asked, "What can we expect next?"

Madam Celeste closed her eyes. "As we all know, Leo, the Dark One, is already at work. We must decipher his plans, counteract his moves." She turned her head to Nick. "Your visions, Nick. Perhaps they can help illuminate Leo's intentions. How do you bring them on?"

Nick shook his head and shrugged his shoulders.. "I don't. I have no control over them at all. They just come in their own time, with no regard for what I want."

For the first time during the meeting, Nate spoke up. "Though they often come on while Nick is working with the tarot. Isn't that right, son?

"Not always, but often, yeah," Nick replied.

"Nick, have you tried using the tarot cards to try to figure out what Leo's planning?" Nate asked. "Perhaps your visions hold the key to understanding Leo's motivations."

Nick shook his head sadly. "No, we decided it was too risky. We didn't know if Leo can follow me or find me through the cards."

Nate furrowed his brow. "Hmm...though perhaps we could try it here at the lodge, with all of us present and protective barriers in place. However, I do agree that it might be best to not touch them when you're alone; we can't risk it. But together, with all of us —"

Helena spoke up firmly. "We've done everything in our power to protect this lodge; with all of us here, I'm certain that Leo won't be able to break through our barriers. Nick should safely be able to use his cards with or without our presence, as long as he does it here."

"I'll try," said Nick, even though he wasn't crazy about attempting to bring on a vision. They usually resulted in excruciating migraines after the fact.

Nick's mother, a tear in her eye, whispered, "How can we help?"

Helena smiled gently. "By understanding, by supporting, and by believing in the strength of light over darkness."

Nick's eyes met Helena's, a burning question clear. "How do we defeat him? Do any of you even have a plan?"

Helena smiled. "It's a blend of strategy and power. We will fortify spiritual hotspots, denying the Dark One access. Then, using rituals and artifacts of old, we hope to weaken him, make him vulnerable."

Sia chimed in, "You, Nick, will be at the heart of this. Your light will counter his darkness, and when the time is right, with all of us by your side, we will seal him away, restoring balance."

Nick's mother, tears forming, whispered, "It's so much for him to bear."

Helena reached out, touching her hand. "Every prophecy, every legend, has its hero. But remember, behind every hero is a loving family, a supportive community. Nick is our hope, but he's also your son. Together, we'll work to ensure he's ready for what lies ahead."

Madam Celeste swiveled her head and locked eyes with Nick's mother. "Oh, and Mrs. Michelson, we urge you to bring your family to stay with us here at the lodge. It's fortified with spiritual protections, and Nick will be closer to us."

Nick's mother crossed her arms, her voice unwavering, "My younger daughter knows nothing about this ghost business, and I intend to keep it that way. I won't expose her to a world she's not prepared for."

Raphael leaned forward. "We understand your reservations, but the stakes have never been higher. With the Dark

One's rising power, no place is truly safe. He may use you to get to Nick."

Nick's mother shook her head. "It's our home. We won't be driven out by fear."

Maya, sensing the rising tension, interjected, "What if we ensured your home's protection while allowing you to stay?"

Curiosity evident in her eyes, Nick's mother asked, "How?"

Eliza, a young witch from the council, stepped forward. "I can stay with you. I'll ensure the wards around your house remain strong and impenetrable.

"And the rest of us will come over to your house and reinforce the protections surrounding it," Helena said. "They'll be the same protections we have here protecting this lodge."

"But how will we explain you?" Nick's mother asked.

"We can say I'm a distant cousin, visiting for a while," Eliza said with a small smile."

Nick's mother looked at Eliza, her defenses softening slightly. "A cousin?"

Maya nodded. "Yes, distant relatives from your mother's side. It will be a believable cover for your daughter, and you'll have an added layer of protection."

She pondered for a moment, then sighed, "Alright. But only if Nick agrees."

Nick nodded appreciatively, "Thank you, Mom."

As the group discussed further details, Nick's mother turned to her son, her eyes filled with concern. "What about Gabriel? Are you worried about him?"

Nick smiled faintly, a mixture of relief and sadness. "It's already taken care of. He'll be safe."

Madam Celeste nodded, then continued, "That's

acceptable. As for the rest of us, we must act fast. Leo may be cunning and resourceful, but we can defeat him.

Nick's mother held up both hands. "Wait! I am still his mother and have a final say about what my son is involved in. Before I agree to anything, I need to know more about this so-called prophecy. You all keep harping on about it, but I've yet to see it. Where is it? What does it say, exactly?"

Madam Celeste opened the manila folder that was next to her. "I have it here." And she began to read:

"In the shadow of Gallowspine where spirits linger and time intertwines,

The Dark One shall rise, from depths of despair, seeking dominion, causing the dead to air.

Power from beyond, to the dead he'll bestow, more potent than the living, a world in throes.

But when darkness peaks and hope seems to wane, from the light shall emerge a counter to the bane.

The Light One will stand, both old and anew, with power and purpose, the world to renew.

Yet victory's not certain, nor is it clear, for Light and Dark will clash, both far and near."

She looked up. "It goes on to talk about the role of the Light One in more detail."

She then resumed reading.

GUARDIAN OF BALANCE*: The Light One — a young but powerful figure destined by fate — is the embodiment of balance in the universe. As both darkness and light exist, the Dark One threatens to upset this equilibrium. Bearing a mysterious mark upon their wrist that has appeared on other Light Ones before them, the Light One is tasked with restoring harmony, preventing either light or dark from over-*

whelming the other. It is their duty to preserve balance, preventing darkness from upsetting the harmony of the cosmos. A daunting task indeed for one so young, but one they must fulfill if the universe is to survive.

PROTECTOR OF THE LIVING*: With the Dark One seeking to empower the dead beyond the living, the Light One is the shield for the living souls. They will prevent the undead from overtaking the realm of the living, safeguarding the natural order of life and death.*

CONDUIT OF SPIRITUAL ENERGY*: The Light One can channel the pure energies from the spiritual realm, making them a formidable force against the Dark One. This connection to the spiritual plane also allows the Light One to communicate and collaborate with benevolent spirits, drawing upon their wisdom and power. With this connection comes visions of future and past events, allowing them to see the course of destiny ahead of its time.*

BEARER OF HOPE*: Beyond just physical or spiritual abilities, the Light One serves as a beacon of hope for all. In times of despair, their presence alone can uplift spirits, rallying forces of good to stand firm against impending darkness.*

SEALER OF THE OTHER SIDE*: One of the gravest threats of the Dark One is his intent to obliterate the Other Side, the realm where spirits find solace after death. The*

Light One has the unique ability to mend and protect this realm, ensuring souls find their deserved peace.

SACRIFICE AND RESURRECTION: *A pivotal part of the prophecy suggests that the Light One might have to make the ultimate sacrifice to thwart the Dark One. Yet, inherent in their role is the cycle of rebirth. While they might fall in the battle against darkness, their essence, spirit, or legacy will always find a way to rise again, continuing the eternal battle between light and dark.*

IN ESSENCE, *the Light One is not just a counter to the Dark One but symbolizes hope, resilience, and the eternal spirit of light that refuses to be extinguished, no matter how overwhelming the darkness might seem.*

AS MADAM CELESTE finished reading the prophecy, a hush of reverence fell over the room, with everyone taking in the gravity of the prophecy. It was as if they were all marveling at the destiny that had been set before them.

Nick's mother sighed and she looked at her son with a mixture of pride and fear in her eyes, as though understanding what he was capable of. With a deep breath, she nodded and said, "Though I still have severe misgivings, I understand now why we need Nick to stand against this Dark One. As much as I would like to, I can't deny my son's destiny."

There was an audible sigh of relief from everyone present as Madam Celeste nodded approvingly. "Very well then," she said. "It is settled. We must make haste and gather our forces before Leo unleashes his unholy power upon us all." With that, they began to strategize their plan of action. They discussed strategies for fighting Leo and how best to use Nick's powers to defeat him. They agreed on tactics for defending themselves against his sinister forces, as well as ways to rally allies from across the world who could join them in their fight. Everyone seemed eager to join in on this mission, and Nick felt a surge of newfound strength within himself, knowing that he had people believing in him and supporting him on his journey ahead.

CHAPTER FOUR

The bell clanged throughout the hallways of Gallowspine Mountains High School, a powerful reverberation that echoed into Nick's ears and made its way down to his feet. A jolt of energy spread through his body as he leapt up from his desk with the rest of his classmates, desperate for lunch break. But before he could join them out the door, something caught his eye — it was a teenage boy, translucent but visible, standing just outside the bustling crowd.

Nick recognized him for what he was immediately—this was no ordinary student. Nick's ability allowed him to see ghosts, and this was one he hadn't seen before. The spectral boy seemed to be around Nick's age and held an aura of profound sadness that made Nick's heart ache. The spectral boy tried catching Nick's gaze, his eyes pleading. As their eyes locked, Nick gave a subtle nod, signaling "Later." The ghost seemed to understand and faded into the background.

Throughout the day, Nick felt a crushing weight on his chest from the image of the ghost that he could not shake off. The sorrow and anguish emanating from the spirit was like an abyssal depth of despair that had taken hold of his soul. When the last bell had finally rung, Nick frantically gathered his things and dashed outside to his trusted spot behind the school; an old tree at the edge of the grounds which he could use as a conduit for spiritual energy, making communication easier.

There, he found the ghost waiting, his form clearer and more present. "You can see me," he whispered, his voice tinged with hope and surprise.

Nick nodded, "I can. My name's Nick. What's yours?"

The ghost hesitated, as if trying to recall a long-lost memory. "Quinn. Quinn Croucher."

Quinn Croucher, even in his spectral form, bore the unmistakable look of a boy caught in the transition between adolescence and young adulthood. Standing at a middling height, he was neither particularly tall nor short, but his slightly hunched shoulders gave the impression of someone carrying more weight than his physical frame suggested.

His skin, a pale luminescent blue, seemed almost translucent, revealing faint outlines of veins, making him even more ethereal. Quinn's face was angular, with high cheekbones and a slightly pronounced jawline. His eyes were a haunting shade of grey, resembling a stormy sky, and always appeared to be shimmering, as if on the verge of tears.

A mop of tousled raven-black hair crowned his head, with unruly strands perpetually falling over his forehead, casting shadows over his eyes. It was clear that in life, this hair would have been the kind that looked like he had just rolled out of bed, effortlessly perfect in its imperfection.

Quinn's attire was a frozen testament to the last moments of his life — a faded graphic tee that clung to his lanky frame, showcasing a band that might've been popular during his time. Over this, he wore a faded leather jacket, which, despite its spectral nature, seemed to hold on to the echoes of its past ruggedness. His jeans, frayed at the edges, looked like they'd seen better days, and his old sneakers, though faded, hinted at many adventures traversed.

While his physical form was undoubtedly captivating, it was Quinn's aura that was most striking. An omnipresent melancholy surrounded him, making the air feel heavier. Yet, amidst this sadness, there was also a flicker of hope, determination, and a yearning for redemption that radiated from his very being.

Nick settled down, leaning against the tree trunk. "Why are you here, Quinn?"

Quinn's face darkened. "I had to get to you, to warn you about Leo. His influence is growing. The afterlife... It's changing. And not for the better."

"Why come to me?"

"You're the Light One, right? Everyone says that you're the only one who can stop him."

Nick straightened. "Okay, tell me everything you know."

Quinn's chest heaved up and down with unnecessary breaths as he spoke. His voice was heavy with urgency, and he paused between each word. "Leo's army... It's not just dark spirits. He's trapping the souls of those trying to cross into the light — convincing them they are unworthy, that punishment and torment await them if they ascend. Their despair, their self-loathing... it feeds Leo and strengthens him."

Nick frowned. "But why? What's his endgame?"

Quinn slowly turned away, his eyes darkening with each deliberate movement. "Dominance," he muttered, "A kingdom of his own making. But more importantly, power.

A power that knows neither borders nor mercy, one that holds sway over both the living and the dead."

"Quinn," Nick spoke in a tense, commanding tone, "you mustn't leave out even the most minuscule detail about Leo. What's his agenda? Why is he going to such lengths?"

The glittering sunlight illuminated Quinn's features, and a vague hint of a smile curved his lips. He paused for a heavy moment, as if collecting eons of memories from a distant past. "Leo's goals aren't simple, Nick," he began softly. "They're the result of ages of resentment and an insatiable thirst for domination that stretches back to a time long before our own."

Nick leaned in, hanging onto every word.

Quinn's voice shook as he spoke, containing a hint of fear in his tone. "First," he continued, his eyes searching back and forth out of nervousness, "he wants to tear down the veil between our world and yours. He dreams of a warped sort of harmony where the dead have control over the living — under his command, an army of undead would reign."

Nick's eyes widened. It's just as the prophecy said. Leo is trying to destroy the Other Side. "So, he's building an army..."

Quinn nodded solemnly. "An army of despair, like a plague that continues to spread. He doesn't just recruit any spirit; he strategically targets the lost, the guilt-ridden, those with regrets. With his silver tongue and devious promises of hope, he convinces them they're unworthy of the light, turning their despair into his power. With every sorrowful spirit, every heartbroken soul filled with regret and guilt, his strength grows — siphoning away their light, until only darkness remains."

Nick shuddered, a chill running down his spine. "I don't get it. Why does he do it? What does he gain?"

Quinn's face darkened with anger and malice, his eyes flashing as he spoke. "Control. It's always about control for him. By disrupting the natural cycle of life, death, and rebirth, he can manipulate the flow of souls, bend them to his will. Imagine being reborn not out of cosmic balance, but because Leo wills it. He aims to be the puppet master of life and afterlife."

Nick's throat was dry as he slowly comprehended the enormity of Leo's scheme. Quinn's tone grew colder as he continued, "He plans to make the dead visible to the living, and then place his spectral legion in positions of power all over the globe over those who have influence — monarchs, dictators, presidents, leaders, anyone with authority. He sees himself ruling both the land of the living and that of the dead."

Nick felt like someone had punched him in the gut at this revelation, his heart thumping wildly against his ribcage. "He wants to rule both worlds."

Quinn's lips pulled into a tight line. He closed his eyes for a moment and heaved a sigh that shook his chest. When he looked up again at Nick, he spoke in measured tones. "Nick, it's not just about ruling. He wants to redraw the boundaries of what's right and wrong, of good and evil — with himself as the final judge. His goal is to create a world with no clear morality, where his word is the only truth."

"I'm not sure if I understand how he could accomplish such a thing."

Quinn continued. "Leo aims to disrupt the natural cycle of life, death, and rebirth. By doing so, he intends to control souls' flow, determining who gets reborn, who remains in limbo, and who serves him. Such control would make him nearly omnipotent, like a deity holding the keys to life and the afterlife.

Nick ran his fingers across his forehead in frustration. "Can you explain to me what Leo is? We've been calling him a demon because we don't know where he came from or what he really is. Is he a demon, a vengeful spirit, or something else entirely?"

"While Leo was alive, he was once a formidable entity in the spiritual realm, his interactions with humans and other spirits led him down a dark path. Long ago, he was like you — an incredibly gifted medium who could speak to the dead. But society did not accept such abilities during that time period and treated him like a pariah — and his community shunned him. Feeling slighted by the natural order of things, he sought more than just dominion over the spectral realm; he coveted influence over the living and the dead and sought revenge over those who had wronged him. So yes, he was once a human and then a spirit. But then he became much more."

A violent silence permeated the air, as if an invisible barrier had been erected. Nick's voice was barely audible when he finally spoke, yet it echoed with a sense of finality. "We have to stop him."

"It's not just about defeating Leo. It's about restoring hope to the countless souls he's ensnared. And there are a lot of them."

As the weight of Quinn's words sank in, Nick wondered aloud, "If Leo's this influential, why come to me? Why didn't you join him?"

Quinn's face contorted with pain. "There are spirits, Nick, who want to help. Not all are swayed by Leo's words. Many of us know about you. Some want to harm you, yes, but some, like me, want to help."

Nick stared at Quinn. "Why didn't you cross over when you had the chance?"

Quinn looked down, shame evident in his eyes. "I wasn't... I wasn't a good person, Nick. When Leo approached me, he played on my fears, made me believe I'd be punished if I tried crossing."

Quinn's head drooped down, and his eyes filled with guilt. "Leo had a way of getting into my head, convincing me that the worst would happen if I defied him, if I ever made an attempt to escape. He knew exactly which buttons to press and convinced me that I would be punished without mercy if I tried to go into the light, that nothing but horrible anguish awaited me. And I believed him."

Nick's heart ached for the lost soul before him. "Quinn, it's never too late to find redemption."

But before Nick could continue, Quinn's form began to waver. "I've stayed too long. I can't let him find me."

Nick reached out, "Wait! Let me help!"

Quinn's voice grew fainter. "Remember, Nick, not all ghosts are your enemy. Some of us still believe in the light. We still believe in you." And with that, he vanished.

Nick sat in silence. The battle ahead was clearer now, not just against dark spirits, but also to save lost souls from their own despair. Determined, Nick stood up, resolute to fight for both the living and the dead.

A sense of urgency wrenched Nick's insides. He had to tell the other psychics about Quinn's vital information. So, with a deep breath and a determined heart, he left school and set off for their location without hesitation. He dreaded what could happen if Leo's scheme were to come to fruition, but he was determined to make a difference. Leo's malicious plan had to be thwarted. Nick sped through the winding streets, his feet pounding along the pavement.

Nick sprinted up to the house, and his heart raced as he spied the faint light coming from his father's study window. He held his breath and tip-toed around the side of the house. Slipping into the garage, Nick let out a relieved sigh that no one had heard him come home. A gentle whisper of exhaust filled the air as he started his scooter and guided it silently away from the house towards the lodge.

CHAPTER FIVE

Nick parked his scooter in the guest parking lot next to the lodge. His breath came out in white puffs as he trudged through the icy air, his shoes crunching over patches of frosted ground. The cold wind nipped at his cheeks as he glanced up at the lodge, its blackened windows staring back like gaping eyes. He quickened his pace and drew up to the entrance, his fingers tightening around his backpack. He opened the door to the vestibule and stepped inside, and felt an eerie stillness overpower him, punctuated only by a faint gust of wind that swept through the chamber. As he approached the main entrance, the door creaked open, revealing an audience of wide-eyed seers who could sense the gravity of the situation. The psychics were gathered before him in a semicircle, their faces illuminated by a single oil lamp hanging from the ceiling. Their expressions were lit up with a mixture of fear and curiosity. They seemed to sense something was wrong — Nick had no doubt that they already knew he was coming.

Nick stepped into the center of the room and looked around, feeling an intense wave of dread wash over him as he noticed how the shadows seemed to flicker around him. He paused for a moment to take in the scene before him, then cleared his throat, trying to ready himself to share with them Leo's sinister plan.

Nate rushed into the room and locked gazes with Nick. "Nick!" he called out, concern etched on his face as he rushed to greet him. "I received your text. What's the matter?"

"Friends, we have no time to waste," Nick began, his voice cracking from the strain of his knowledge. His hands trembled as he spoke. "Leo is planning something far worse than we ever imagined. I've learned more about Leo's endgame from a ghost named Quinn. We're not just up against a power-hungry spirit; we're facing a threat that could change the very fabric of existence."

A murmur rippled through the room, the psychics exchanging uneasy glances. Nick took a deep breath and continued, trying to keep his voice steady.

"His primary goal is to blur the veil between the living and the dead." Nick's hands moved around wildly. "He wants to create a world where spirits and humans coexist, but not harmoniously." He paused for a moment, allowing the weight of his words to sink in. "In this new world, the dead would hold sway, leading the living based on Leo's commands."

The psychics gasped, their faces contorted with horror. Nick knew they understood the implications all too well; if Leo succeeded, they would lose their unique connection to the spirit world, becoming mere playthings for the malevolent forces that lurked beyond the veil.

"It's just as the prophecy foretold," said Madame Celeste.

"Leo has been targeting lost, regretful souls," Nick

continued, eyes darting from one face to another. "He convinces them of their unworthiness, turning them into powerful entities filled with hate and despair. This army of despair amplifies his power—he feeds off their sorrow, guilt, and hopelessness."

"An army of the dead?" whispered Paola, a frail psychic in the back, her hands trembling. "How would we even begin to fight such a force?" Others echoed her sentiment, their voices raw with fear.

Nick shook his head, his brow furrowed. "I don't know, but we gotta find a way, right?" He paused, taking a deep breath before continuing. "Oh, and get this. Leo aims to disrupt the natural cycle of life, death, and rebirth. He wants to determine who gets reborn, who remains in limbo, and who serves him. It's like he's trying to turn himself into a god."

A collective gasp echoed through the Lodge.

"And he could do it, too," Madame Celeste said. "With control over reincarnation, Leo would hold the keys to both life and afterlife, making him nearly omnipotent."

"Furthermore," Nick continued, trying to speak as quickly as he could, "with his spectral army and control over reincarnation, Leo plans to influence the realm of the living: monarchs, presidents, leaders, politicians, influencers — anyone of power would be subtly or overtly controlled by his spiritual minions."

"Then we must act swiftly," said Nate, his voice steady despite the look of panic on his face. "We cannot allow this demon to bring his twisted vision to fruition. Remember — we're fighting not only for ourselves but for the countless souls caught in Leo's web." He held up a finger in the air. "You said that Leo feeds off the despair, guilt, and hopeless-ness of regretful souls. Understanding this dynamic is crucial. We must develop a method to either cleanse these emotions from the souls Leo controls or redirect these emotions in a way that weakens him, rather than strengthens him."

As the psychics began to brainstorm, Nick grappled with his own fears and doubts. Would they really be able to thwart Leo's sinister ambitions? Or would they fall victim to his dark influence?

"We'll have to pool all our resources," suggested a young psychic, whose name Nick had forgotten. Her eyes burned fiercely with determination. "We must find a way to counteract Leo's control over reincarnation and weaken his influence over the living."

"Yes, Leo's plan to control reincarnation is particularly alarming," Madam Celeste said. "To prevent this, I suggest we research ancient rituals and seek allies with knowledge of life and death cycles to protect or shield the process of reincarnation from Leo's influence."

"Yes, we have to bring in others," said another, clenching his fists in resolve. "We have to reach out to our allies, both in this world and beyond. I've read of others even contacting entities from other dimensions who have a vested interest in maintaining the balance between life and death. I'll begin researching this right away."

"How about researching Leo?" Nick asked.

Madame Celeste tapped her chin with her forefinger. "What do you mean?"

"If he's a spirit, then he must have been a human at one time, right? Maybe researching the human Leo might give us some insight into his motivations."

"Good thinking, Nick. Jasper and I will see what we can find. I learned that there are a couple of occult bookshops in the nearby town. It might not hurt to pay them a visit."

"And we should focus on creating a safe haven," said Maya who had been quiet until now. "A protected area or a sanctuary where neither Leo nor his minions can reach could serve both as a base for operations and a refuge for endangered souls."

"That's brilliant!" Nate said. "This would allow those souls who defect from Leo to find safety. Between all of us, we should easily be able to raise up a powerful protective boundary. The more souls who seek refuge with us, the more Leo will weaken."

Nick felt a flicker of hope. United together, the psychics were a formidable force — one that he believed could stand against Leo's malevolent tide.

Madame Celeste raised both of her hands and everyone stopped talking. "Above all, we must concentrate on unlocking Nick's hidden powers. Our Light One is young and untried, but that mustn't stop us from fighting with everything we have. But our dear Nick faces a monumental challenge. We are in the realm of the Dark One; he has gained strength and power over decades, perhaps centuries and more so recently. No matter what we do or how we strategize, the old texts say that ultimately, it will be up to the Light One to vanquish the Dark One. Nick is capable; we've all sensed it. We just need to find the way to help him discover it."

"But how?" Nick asked.

Madame Celeste stepped forward and settled her gaze on Nick. "We will help you unlock your powers," she announced solemnly. "And I believe I know where we should start." She looked at several of the psychics in the room and continued, "You should offer yourselves to work with Nick — to assist him on this journey."

The psychics in the room seemed to brighten at her suggestion and they bustled around Nick, introducing themselves with eagerness. Some offered spiritual guidance, while others bragged about their focus or offered to teach Nick how to maximize his newfound abilities.

Nick's heart and mind raced as he listened and surveyed the group. He still wasn't sure what they could do against Leo's army, so he turned to Madame Celeste with a pleading look. "Can this even work?" he asked.

Madame Celeste smiled reassuringly. "My dear Nick," she said, her face radiating assurance. "Just like Leo has tapped into dark magic, you too can wield the power of light and life to take on his forces. But only you — the Light One — can stand toe-to-toe against such darkness without being corrupted himself." She paused for a moment, then added with a hint of a smile, "But if we all stand together, I know that you will triumph over Leo's forces."

Nick steeled himself for the challenge and nodded in agreement to their plan of action; despite his fears, he was determined to fight.

CHAPTER SIX

NICK'S DREAMS HAD ALWAYS BEEN VIVID, BUT LATELY, they'd taken on a new level of intensity. It was as if he were living an entirely separate existence in his sleep, one that was just as real — and sometimes more so — than the life he lived when he was awake.

Tonight, as Nick lay in bed, his consciousness drifted into darkness. His body grew weightless, and he sensed himself floating through an endless void.

"Hello?"

The voice startled Nick, causing him freeze up. He looked around, but there was nobody there — nothing but swirls of mist.

"Is somebody there?" the voice asked again. It sounded distant, like an echo from another time.

Suddenly, a wall of light appeared before him, like a glowing curtain drawn across the ether. And behind it, another world materialized. It was a room — small, dimly lit, cluttered with objects that seemed to straddle the line between antiques and junk.

"Where am I?" Nick murmured aloud, even though he

understood instinctively that this was not a dream. This was something else. Perhaps a vision.

"Ricky's Emporium of the Occult" read a sign on the wall. Nick glanced around again, taking in the myriad of artifacts that filled the space. There were old books with cracked leather bindings, tarnished silver chalices, crystal balls, pentagrams, and talismans of every shape and size.

"Who's there?" a voice demanded suddenly, causing Nick to jump. "Show yourself! I command it!"

A figure emerged from the shadows, his eyes widening in shock. He stood at a height similar to Nick's, with tousled dark hair falling over his forehead and a neatly trimmed beard framing his angular jawline. His gaze scanned Nick's face, taking in every detail before finally resting on his eyes. The boy appeared to be around Nick's age, perhaps a year or two older, with a determined expression on his face.

"Who.... are you?" Nick replied, his voice cracking with uncertainty.

"Ricky," the boy said. "I didn't expect to find anyone here. Usually, I get a warning before someone shows up."

"Here? Where is here, exactly?" Nick demanded, trying to maintain some semblance of control over this dream — or vision — or whatever in the hell it was.

"Inside my mind," Ricky replied nonchalantly, as if it were the most natural thing in the world." Ricky narrowed his eyes at Nick. "You seem different from the others."

"What others?"

"Spirits," Ricky said hesitantly. "You seem much more vivid than the other spirits who come. Do you remember how you died?"

"Uh, no," Nick replied, shaking his head. "I'm very much alive."

"Alive?" The young man frowned, clearly puzzled. He

shook his head. "I'm so sorry. You probably don't remember what happened to you. You see, I only ever speak with those who've crossed over and since you're in my mind, you must be dead."

"Dead?" Nick spluttered, disbelief and fear sending his heart into overdrive. "No, no, I'm alive! I'm ... dreaming, I think."

"Ha!" the man snorted, though there was no humor in his eyes. "Dreaming? And yet you managed to find your way into my mind? Unlikely."

"Your... mind?" Nick echoed, understanding dawning on him. "I'm not really sure how I got here, to be honest. So, are you like a wizard or something?"

The boy chuckled. "I'm actually a psychic medium. My name is Ricky. And if you're not really dead, then it seems you've somehow entered my channeling. What's your name?"

"Nick," he responded, extending his hand. "Nice to meet you, Ricky."

Ricky hesitated for a moment before shaking Nick's hand. "Likewise. But how is this possible? How can you be here if you're not a spirit?"

"Look, I'm confused how I ended up here, but I assure you, I'm not dead," Nick insisted. A cold sweat broke out across his brow. "It might have something to do with the fact that I'm also a psychic medium. I can't channel like you, though. I only see the spirits in the real world who haven't crossed over yet. But sometimes I get visions of the past and future."

"Interesting," Ricky mused, stroking his beard thoughtfully. "I've never met another psychic medium like myself, let alone one who was able to enter my mental space like this."

"Same here," Nick agreed. "So you can see dead people in your mind?"

Ricky nodded. "I contact the dead once they have crossed over," Ricky explained. "It's not something I always can control, though. They come to me when they have unfinished business or need help with something in the physical world. My gift allows me to communicate with them and help those who are still living find closure or answers. Usually it's the living who contacts me, trying to get in touch with a loved one who's crossed over."

"Wow," Nick breathed, feeling a pang of envy. "I wish I could do that. All I get are the ones who haven't crossed over yet."

"Thank you," Ricky replied, a faint blush coloring his cheeks. "However, I must admit, your ability to interact with spirits before they cross over is equally fascinating. I've never seen a spirit outside of my mind. How did you discover your gift?"

"I had it for a while before I even realized it. I'd see ghosts all the time but didn't realize that they were spirits — often, they resemble real people and when they do, it's difficult to tell the difference." Nick grinned wryly. "My uncle, who was also a medium, told me what I was seeing and helped me understand my ability."

"Same for me, except it was my Gran." He creased his brow. "As bizarre as this whole situation is, I suppose there's no harm in trying to make sense of it together."

"Thanks, Ricky." Relief washed over Nick like a warm wave, and he allowed himself a small smile.

"But enough about me," Ricky said. "How did you end up here, anyway?"

"I have no idea. I was just lying in bed, and the next thing I knew, I was in this... place."

"Hmm...perhaps our gifts are linked somehow," Ricky mused. "Like two sides of the same coin."

"Possibly," Nick agreed, intrigued by the possibility. "I mean, we're both mediums, right? That might be why we're able to connect like this."

"Seems plausible," Ricky concurred. He tapped his chin thoughtfully, blue eyes flicking back and forth as if reading some invisible text. "Well, first things first: we need to determine if this is actually a dream or something more... tangible. Can you experience pain in this place?"

"Uh, I'm not sure," Nick admitted, glancing down at his bare feet on the carpeting. "I haven't tried."

"Give it a go," Ricky suggested, nodding towards a large hunk of bark on his desk.

"Pick that up and see if you can feel the roughness of the bark or the sting of a splinter."

"Alright." With a deep breath, Nick stepped forward and pressed his palm against the gnarled bark. He could feel every ridge and furrow beneath his fingertips, the sensation so vivid that he couldn't help but wince when a particularly sharp edge dug into his skin.

"Ouch!" he yelped, pulling his hand away and examining the tiny droplet of blood welling up from the wound. "Yeah, I'd say this seems pretty real to me."

"Curious," Ricky mused, his gaze intent on Nick's injured hand. "So if this isn't a dream, then what is it? Some sort of shared psychic space?"

"That's an interesting theory," Nick agreed, both intrigued and unnerved by the possibilities. "But how do we find out for sure? And more importantly, how do we get back to our own minds?"

"Damned fine question."

As they continued to speak, Nick couldn't help but

perceive a sense of camaraderie with Ricky. For the first time in his life, he'd met someone his own age who truly understood what it was like to walk between the worlds of the living and the dead.

"Wait a minute," Ricky interrupted suddenly, a look of concern crossing his face. "If you're in my mind, does that mean you can see everything I'm thinking? All my memories and secrets?"

"Uh, no!" Nick reassured him quickly. "I promise. I don't have access to your thoughts or anything like that. I'm just... here, with you."

"Good," Ricky said, visibly relieved. "Not that I have anything to hide, mind you, but the idea of someone snooping around in my head is a bit unsettling."

"Understandable," Nick agreed. "And to be honest, I'd prefer not to invade anyone's privacy like that either. But it seems we've stumbled upon something extraordinary here — two mediums from different realms connecting like this."

"Indeed," Ricky nodded. "Perhaps we met for a reason. There must be some purpose behind our connection."

"There might be," Nick mused. "But for now, at least, let's just enjoy the fact that we're not alone in our abilities. It's nice to know there's someone else out there who understands. I'm in contact right now with a bunch of other psychics, but they're way older than me. It's nice to have someone around my age."

"Agreed," Ricky smiled. "And who knows? Perhaps we'll find a way to use our abilities together one day — maybe even team up."

"Wouldn't that be cool?" Nick replied, returning the smile. "So, what do we do now? Do we just, uh, hang out in your mind for a while?"

"Beats me," Ricky admitted with a shrug. "But we can figure it out as we go along."

"Fair enough," Nick agreed. "Do you want to try contacting one of the dead people you've channeled before?"

"Sure," Ricky said, excitement clear in his voice. "I'd love to show you what I do. Hold on, let me see if I can find someone."

There was a moment of silence as Ricky presumably searched his mental archives for a suitable spirit, though Nick had no idea how it all worked. He held his breath, unsure of what to expect.

"Got someone!" Ricky announced triumphantly. "Her name's Sarah. She died a couple of years ago, but she still visits me from time to time."

"Can I talk to her?" Nick asked eagerly.

"Go ahead," Ricky prompted, stepping aside to allow Nick access to Sarah's spectral presence.

"Hello, Sarah?" Nick called out hesitantly, feeling slightly ridiculous.

"Who's this?" a soft, feminine voice replied, sounding somewhat confused.

"Nick," he answered quickly. "I'm a friend of Ricky's."

"Ah," Sarah said, sounding relieved. "Someone new. It's nice to meet you, Nick."

"Likewise," Nick replied politely. "So, how does this work? Can you tell me anything about the other side?"

"Unfortunately, I can't," Sarah said apologetically. "I'm not allowed to reveal too much. But I can tell you it's a beautiful place, full of peace and love."

"Sounds wonderful," Nick murmured wistfully.

"It is," Sarah confirmed. "But I'm sure you have plenty

of time left on Earth, so don't worry about crossing over just yet. It was nice talking to you, Nick"

"Thanks," Nick said, trying to sound cheerful. "I hope we'll meet again someday."

"Perhaps," she agreed, her voice fading away like a whisper on the wind. Then she was gone.

"Wow, that was incredible," Nick gushed once Sarah had departed. "I've experienced nothing like that before."

"Neither have I," Ricky admitted. "But now that we learned it's possible, we can explore this connection further."

"Um...Ricky," Nick began, his voice steady but his heart heavy with emotion, "I need to ask you something serious. Have you ever heard of Leo?"

Ricky furrowed his brow. "Leo? I don't think so. Is he another psychic medium?"

Nick shook his head. "No, he's kind of a shadow demon who's been murdering psychic mediums."

Ricky's eyebrows shot up, his eyes widening as shock washed over his features. "Yikes!" he replied, concern seeping into his voice. "No, I haven't. Why do you ask? Have you encountered this...Leo?"

"Unfortunately, yes," Nick admitted, rubbing his temples as if trying to ward off a headache. "It's a long story, but I've had one run-in with him, and now I'm kind of in his crosshairs. He's extremely dangerous, Ricky, and he seems to have a vendetta against people like us."

Ricky's face paled, and he swallowed hard, visibly shaken by the revelation. "What does he want?" he asked, his once confident demeanor now replaced by fear.

"We're not entirely sure," Nick lied. A shiver ran down his spine just thinking about the malevolent force he'd faced. "But whatever it is, it can't be good. That's why I think that maybe you and I need to meet up in person so I can fill you in on everything I know."

"Meet up? Like, in real life?" Ricky hesitated, uncertainty flickering in his eyes. "But how can we even do that? We don't even know where each other lives. We might live on opposite sides of the globe."

"I live in Gallowspine Mountains," Nick said. "How about you?"

"Now that is a coincidence. I live a little over an hour away."

"I'd like to get together and talk, if you're up for it" Nick said, then a heaviness tugged at his chest.

"Wait," Nick said.

"Yeah?"

"On second thought, I'm not sure if it's a good idea. You see, that shadow demon has specifically been targeting me. It's a long story, but maybe it wouldn't be safe for you to be with me. I don't want him to find out about you." As Nick stared at Ricky, he wondered whether Ricky might be gay. But then again, what did it matter? Nick's heart belonged to Gabe, and nothing would ever change that.

Ricky seemed to weigh the options in his mind, his expression a mix of fear and determination. "No," he finally said, meeting Nick's gaze with steely resolve. "You're right. We need to understand what we're up against so we can protect ourselves and others like us. If this demon is hunting psychic mediums, then we have to do everything in our power to stop him and I need to know more about him. I'm in. Let's meet."

"Thank you," Nick breathed, relief washing over him like a warm wave. He didn't tell Ricky about the team of psychics already here and looking into it. That could wait until they meet in person. "We'll figure something out, I promise. A bunch of us are working on it."

"Alright," Ricky said, steeling himself and looking at Nick with determination. "Let's do this. When and where do you want to get together?"

"Are you familiar with the Café Viking?"

"Yup. I've been there with my parents a few times."

"How about next Saturday, say around 3:00?" Nick asked.

Ricky smiled. "Sounds perfect. I'm looking forward to meeting you in person. This is going to be so cool. It'll be the first time I've ever met with another medium."

"Uh-oh," said Ricky. "Something's happening. I'm losing you."

"Take care, Ricky," Nick whispered, sensing the dream-world slip away from him as consciousness beckoned.

"Until we meet again, Nick," Ricky replied, his voice echoing in the shrinking space between them.

And with that, the connection severed, leaving Nick once again alone in his room.

CHAPTER SEVEN

"Nick, honey, can you come in here for a minute?"

Nick's ears perked up at the faint sound of his mother's voice reverberating through the walls. With a sigh, he paused his video game and reluctantly dragged himself out of his room. The familiar scent of freshly brewed coffee filled his nose as he entered the living room, where his mom sat on the edge of the sofa, a worried expression etched into her features. He was aware of the tension in the air as she nervously fidgeted with her hands.

Nick couldn't help but notice her untouched coffee mug on the table, the aroma of fresh brew still lingering in the air. "What's going on, Mom?" he asked, eager to learn what had disrupted their evening routine.

"Honey, I just got off the phone with my dear friend Bree McDermott. You remember her, don't you? She's been struggling with some major issues lately, specifically with her son, Ryan." Every word that came out of Nick's mother's mouth was laced with tension and anxiety, her wringing hands a clear indication of her internal turmoil. "Do you know him?"

"Ryan? Of course. We've been classmates for years and we even used to hang out when we were little," Nick replied. He furrowed his brow as he searched his memory for any recent interactions with the other boy. "He's always been kind of a jerk, but lately, it seems like he's been causing more trouble than usual. The teachers seem pretty fed up with him." Nick turned down the corners of his lip in a frown, thinking back on some of Ryan's antics that had caused chaos and disruption in their classes.

"His father's recent passing may have taken a toll on his behavior," his mother sighed, her eyes reflecting both sadness and concern. "He took it pretty hard, from what Bree told me."

"I remember that. He was out of school for quite some time."

"But this isn't about that," she said, straightening out imaginary creases on her pants. "Bree confided in me that Ryan claims there have been strange occurrences in his room — whispering, objects moving without explanation. While she was talking to me, I wondered if this was one of *your* types of special situations. If it is, I fear for both of them."

Nick's tone was dripping with doubt as he responded, not even bothering to hide his skepticism. "Seriously? Are you sure Ryan isn't just trying to get attention or cause trouble like he always does at school?" He rolled his eyes. The kid was an ace number one prick these days. "I'd find it difficult to believe anything he says."

"But it's possible," she admitted, "but then again, perhaps not. What if there *is* something strange going on? Like..." Her voice trailed off, and she hesitated before continuing. "Well, I hate to say it, but ... what if it's a ghost?"

Nick shrugged. "I suppose it's possible. It wouldn't be the first time that a ghost has shown up at a classmate's house."

Her hands trembled as she spoke, the worry in her voice clear. "I realize you're not supposed to be helping ghosts, but I'm truly concerned for Bree and her son. You should have heard her. She was so upset and said she was at wit's end." She sighed. "Maybe you could pop in and do a quick sweep to ensure it's not a spirit? And if it is, you don't have to engage with it. In fact, I don't want you to." She turned to face him, her eyes pleading. "We only need to understand what we're dealing with so we can help them. If there is a spirit present, we'll figure out a way to remove it from the house without involving you directly. I'm sure your psychic friends would know what to do. Please, it shouldn't hurt to at least take a look, right?" Her voice rose an octave in her earnestness.

Nick let out a sigh, sensing her worry for her friend Bree and her son Ryan. The image of a young Ryan attending one of his birthday parties years ago flashed through his mind, spurring him to a decision.

"Fine," Nick sighed, a mix of amusement and concern for his mother's friend washing over him. "I'll go over to Bree and Ryan's house and see what's going on with Ryan. But you'll have to come up with a good reason for me to go there without mentioning ghosts. I don't want anyone else at school to learn about what I can do, especially Ryan McDermott."

"Thank you, sweetie," his mom replied, relief washing over her face. "I'll work on coming up with a good excuse.

Perhaps I can tell her you two need to work on a school project together, or something like that."

Nick shook his head. "Nah, that wouldn't work. Ryan and I rarely communicate at school and we don't run in the same circles. He'd suspect something was up, for sure."

"You can tell him you forgot to copy down the homework and ask him for the assignment? I dunno. I'll think of something and talk to her. I know. Maybe we'll tell her that you're taking teen peer counseling training? That might work."

"Sounds like a plan," Nick agreed, giving his mom a reassuring smile. At least he'd be able to put her mind at ease, even if this business turned out to be nothing more than Ryan's wild imagination or a desperate attempt for attention. Or Ryan just being a dick, as usual.

"Do you want me to come with you when you go?" she asked as she scribbled something down on the paper.

"No, I'll handle it myself," Nick replied. "Unless you want to come and play mediator between Ryan and me."

"No need," his mother chuckled. "I trust you can handle him yourself. You've dealt with worse things than a rowdy teenager."

"True that."

A mix of excitement and trepidation overwhelmed Nick at the thought of visiting Bree's house. It's true Ryan was a jerk, but what if there really was something odd happening in his room? What would he do then? And what if it drew Leo to the house? Hell, what if it *was* Leo?

"Mom, are you sure this is a good idea?" he asked a few moments later, unable to shake off the nagging doubt that had been plaguing him.

The soft, reassuring tone in her voice calmed the anxious flutter in his chest. She gently placed a hand on his shoulder, a comforting gesture that made him feel less alone.

"Sweetie," she said, her eyes filled with concern, "all I'm asking is for you to check things out for our own peace of mind." Her fingers lightly grazed his shoulder, as if to further soothe his worries. A faint aroma of lavender emanated from her skin. "If there's nothing going on, then you can tell me, and we can both put this behind us. But if something strange is happening, then at least we'll know, and we can figure out what to do from there. Perhaps even consult your friends at the lodge, if need be." The soft candlelight danced across her face, casting shadows that added an air of mystery to her words. He couldn't help but be drawn in by her gentle touch and persuasive words, but a subtle unease lingered in the back of his mind, warning him that there was more to this situation than met the eye.

Nick's agreement came with a slow nod. His mother made a valid point. And deep down, he understood that if he could ease his mother's friend's fears, it would bring him a sense of fulfillment and purpose, especially given how powerless he's been feeling these days.

"Good," his mom smiled, squeezing his shoulder gently before standing up. "Now, let's enjoy our dinner and not worry about any of this ghost business until we have to."

"Deal," Nick replied, forcing a smile onto his face as he stood up and walked toward the dining room table. After all, what were the chances of there actually being a ghost in Ryan's room? It was probably just another one of the kid's pranks. And if it wasn't... well...Nick would figure out something.

His mother disappeared into the kitchen and returned a moment later with a pan of bubbly lasagna in one hand and a plate of garlic bread in the other. It was only Nick and his mother for dinner as his father was working late at the university and his sister, Missy, was at a friend's house.

The delicious aroma of the dinner filled the air, and Nick's stomach growled in anticipation. His mom dished out generous portions onto their plates, and they dug in. The comforting flavors melted in his mouth, and he appreciated having such a wonderful mother who cooked like a pro.

As they ate, they chatted about school and work, trying to push away the unsettling thoughts about Ryan's room. Nick's mom kept the conversation light and positive, asking him about his classes and any plans for the weekend. He noticed she avoided any discussion about the psychics or the demon that stalked them. Nick did remind her that "cousin" Eliza would be coming tomorrow to stay with them so they would need to come up with an explanation for Missy.

But despite her best efforts to keep the conversation light, Nick could not shake off the unsettling sensation that had been creeping up on him all day. He tried to brush it off as just nerves about checking out Ryan's room, but there was something else gnawing at him — a sense of foreboding that he couldn't quite place.

After dinner, they cleared the table together and washed the dishes while chatting casually. Once everything was clean and put away, Nick retreated to his room to finish some homework while his mom settled onto the couch with a book.

He opened the door to his room. The walls were a jumble of color, and a motley collection of posters ranging from classic rock bands to obscure art prints adorned them. A bulky, slightly outdated computer monitor, which he plugged into his laptop, occupied a considerable portion of his desk, surrounded by scattered papers, dog-eared textbooks, and a small, rebellious cactus struggling in a sun-starved corner.

His unmade bed rested against the far wall, its navy blue comforter tangled in a disarray, evidence that he'd left in haste that morning. Various keepsakes — a mix of novels, comic books, and forgotten school projects — crammed the shelves above the bed. On the nightstand beside his bed, amidst the usual detritus of snack wrappers, rested his trusty tarot deck. These cards, a gift from his deceased uncle, sparked a touch of the mystical amidst the ordinary chaos of his room.

He sat down at his desk and flipped open his U.S. Government book to study for tomorrow's quiz. He stared blankly at the textbook for what seemed like hours before finally giving up and flopping back onto his bed with a sigh. His mind continuously wandered back to Ryan and Bree's house — what might be taking place there? Was it really only a silly prank on Ryan's part or was there something more supernatural at play?

He rolled over onto his side and closed his eyes, trying to clear his mind. But instead of finding peace in sleep, uneasy dreams filled with ghostly apparitions and ominous whispers plagued him.

It wasn't until he heard a gentle knocking on his door that he woke up with a start. His mom peeked her head inside with a sympathetic smile.

"Sorry sweetie," she said softly, "I didn't mean to wake you."

Nick rubbed his eyes sleepily and sat up, experiencing disorientation and a sense of unease.

"It's okay, Mom," he replied, trying to shake off the residual fear from his dreams.

"I just wanted to check in on you. I know everything

that's going on right now is probably weighing heavily on your mind."

Nick sighed and nodded, grateful for his mom's understanding. "I just took a little nap, is all."

She sat down next to him on the bed and put a comforting hand on his shoulder. "I know it's hard, honey. But we'll get through all of this together. I promise."

Nick managed a small smile before getting up and stretching.

"I think I'm gonna go for a walk," he announced suddenly.

His mom raised an eyebrow but didn't object. He followed her downstairs.

"Be careful," she warned as Nick quickly grabbed his jacket and headed out the door.

The cool night air felt refreshing against his skin as he walked down the quiet neighborhood streets. He found himself irresistibly compelled towards Ryan's house — like a bear to honey. Despite his better judgment, he stood in front of the darkened windows, staring up at the second-floor bedroom.

Suddenly, Nick's stomach lurched, signaling a spirit nearby. Nick spun around but saw nothing.

"Hello?" he called out tentatively into the silent darkness.

But there was no answer — only an eerie silence that made Nick's skin crawl. He glanced around again, surveying his surroundings. With a deep breath, he turned on his heels and headed back to his own house. Whatever mystery there was in Ryan's house would have to wait for another day.

CHAPTER EIGHT

NICK CHOSE A SEAT IN THE CORNER OF THE WARM, bustling coffee shop, the clamor of grinding beans and chattering voices mingling with the scent of freshly baked goods. He glanced around, noting the steamy windows fogged by the contrast of the cold winter air outside against the cozy atmosphere within. It was the agreed upon meeting spot for him and Nate, one where they could comfortably discuss the supernatural world without drawing too much attention to themselves and away from the tense, chaotic atmosphere of the lodge. Despite the noise, there was a comforting sense of privacy.

"Hey, Nick!" Nate greeted, sliding into the seat across from Nick, his eyes bright and welcoming. He was a tall, thin man with a mop of curly brown hair that always seemed to defy gravity. His face was angular yet friendly, with a wide, infectious smile that made it hard not to like him. Nate's presence often put people at ease, which was helpful given his abilities as a psychic.

"Hey, Nate," Nick replied, offering a half-smile in

return. "So, what's going on? You sounded pretty urgent on the phone. Have there been any breakthroughs?"

Nate leaned forward, his elbows resting on the table, his hands clasped together. "I've been talking to some of the other psychics, and we keep encountering the same thing. Every ghost we come across keeps mentioning two people: the Light One and the Dark One."

Nick's heart thumped, a sense of unease settling within him. "And you all really, really still think that I'm the Light One? Are you sure? Like there's no doubt whatsoever? Not even an eensy-weensy bit?"

Nate let out a soft chuckle and shook his head. Nate stated, "You heard all that was said when we met with everyone and went over the prophecy. Everything we've learned points to you and Leo being the ones these ghosts are talking about, though they are hesitant to say your names, especially Leo's. Probably fearful they'll invoke him or draw his attention. But they all agree that one can save us, and the other can bring devastation. And from what we've seen, it's obvious which side you fall on."

Nick rubbed his temples, trying to process the overwhelming information. "You all keep telling me I'm the Light One and I have this mark to prove it. I'll buy that. But... but why me? I'm just... me. A nobody." He let out a sigh, overwhelmed by his own insignificance in the presence of such grandiose assertions.

Nate's gaze was unwavering as he spoke softly, his words carrying a weight of conviction. "Because, Nick," he said, his voice laced with gentle understanding. "In all my years as a psychic, I've met no one who radiates light the way you do. Your aura is like a beacon of hope and comfort to those around you. You possess an incredible ability to uplift and inspire others, even in the darkest of times. You're special, regardless of whether you realize it. And I believe in you. We all believe in you."

"Um..thanks."

"It's not just your strong connection to the spirit world," Nate suggested, his voice tinged with awe. "Besides your innate ability to communicate with ghosts, you possess the rare gift of seeing past, present, and future events. Your visions. Trust me when I say that there are very few who can do what you can do, Nick, if any at all." Nate sucked in a deep breath. "And let's not forget about the light that emanates from your hands," he added, referencing Nick and Gabe's previous encounter with Leo. "That's a power unlike anything I've ever heard of before. We still haven't figured out what it is."

"Perhaps you all are right," Nick conceded, though he still found it difficult to accept. "But how can you be so sure that I'm not the Dark One? What if I'm the one who brings destruction?"

Nate let out a small laugh and shook his head. "No, Nick. That's not possible. Everything we've seen from you has been about helping people, about making the world a better place. Katrina told me about all the lives you've touched and the good deeds you've done, all the people and spirits you've helped." As Nate spoke, images flashed through Nick's mind — the grateful smiles of those he had helped, the sense of purpose and fulfillment he experienced every time he made a difference.

"And even when you faced Leo and his darkness," Nate continued, "you stood firm against him. Your unwavering determination and strength weakened his grip in the real world and you drove him off. That's something to be proud of." With each word from Nate, a glimmer of hope rekin-dled within Nick. Perhaps there was something greater meant for him — something good and noble.

"Even though I'm not sure how I drove Leo off," Nick said slowly, biting his lip as he considered the implications. "It just kind of happened. But I'll go with it and assume you guys are right. I have to. But I still don't know how I'm supposed to fight him. Has anyone come up with anything?"

"Not yet, but we will," Nate replied. "First, we need to learn as much as we can about the Light One and the Dark One. There has to be some specific reason why all eyes are on you now, at this moment. Why every ghost we encounter seems to be focused on you and Leo. It's as if the entire other side knows what Leo is planning and is holding their breath until the two of you meet on the battlefield. They all say that a showdown will be inevitable, but beyond that, they know nothing else. Except for what your ghost friend told you...Quentin, was it?"

"Quinn."

"Ah yes, Quinn. Beyond what he shared with you, we don't know any of the specifics. But we're getting there."

"Right," Nick agreed, sensing a newfound determination building up inside him. "If I really am this Light One, then I'll do whatever it takes to protect the people I love and stop Leo.

Nate smiled warmly. "I know we can count on you, Nick."

"Of course," Nick replied, his voice barely more than a whisper. As he looked around the coffee shop, the world outside seemed far away, quiet and distant compared to the chaos that now resided within him.

"Would you like to get a bite to eat? I recall you telling me that their sandwiches here are superb."

Nick shook his head. "I can't. I'm meeting Gabe for lunch."

Nate arched his eyebrows in surprise. "So I take it you haven't been able to convince him to leave town?"

Nick let out a heavy sigh, his shoulders slumping. "I've been trying, but he's being stubborn. He has this crazy notion that he needs stay here to protect me. I'm not sure what to do. One minute he says he'll go, and the next he insists on staying by my side. It's beyond frustrating."

Nate offered a consoling squeeze on Nick's shoulder. "He just cares about you and wants to make sure you're safe. You can't fault the boy for that." He offered a hopeful smile. "Let's hope he realizes it's better for both of you if he leaves." The weight of Nate's hand reassured him.

Nick's voice trembled as he spoke, his eyes darting nervously around the room and fingers tapping against the smooth surface of the wooden table. "I don't know what I'd do if something happened to Gabe," he admitted in a shaky whisper.

Nate's face softened with genuine concern. "Let's hope it never comes to that. But you must keep trying to get him to leave. It's the only way to be sure of his safety." He took a slow sip from his drink, the ice clinking against the glass before he set it down on the table with a gentle thud. "Will you be stopping by the lodge later?"

Nick nodded, his brow furrowed. "I have a few hours of training scheduled for later."

"And how's your training progressing?" Nate leaned in, genuinely interested.

"It's been...fine, I suppose." Nick's shoulders slumped slightly and his voice became more subdued. "Exhausting, though. I've induced a couple of short visions, but unfortunately, they've provided no new information about Leo. But I won't give up."

His friend patted him on the back reassuringly. "That's all we can ask for."

~

THE ENTICING AROMA OF GREASY, fried food enveloped the air as Nick pushed through the glass door of his and Gabe's favorite burger joint. In the bustling ambiance of the local cafe, Nick stepped into the dining room, his eyes scanning the room until they settled on his boyfriend Gabe, who sat casually at their favorite table by the window. Gabe, with his striking blond hair and easy smile, looked up and caught Nick's gaze. A small, knowing smile spread across Gabe's face as he waved subtly.

Nick responded with a quick, affectionate gesture of his own before he headed to the counter. The staff greeted him with familiar nods; no words were needed as they already knew to whip up two burgers and a side of fries — the duo's usual order. The sizzle of the grill in the background and the aroma of cooking food filled the air, adding a layer of comfort and expectation to their routine.

With the order placed then received, Nick walked over to the table, his steps quick with anticipation. Nick sat across from Gabe and held the tray of wrapped burgers. "Lunch is served."

"You're late," Gabe said, a wry smirk on his face.

"Sorry," Nick replied, setting down the tray. "I was at the coffee shop with Nate." He handed Gabe his burger and fries, then took a sip of his soda. As they ate, he couldn't help but feel a little nervous about what he was going to tell Gabe.

Gabe shook his head. "Two cafes in one day? Why you're little 'ol dance card is full to the brim these days."

"That's an understatement."

"Something on your mind?" Gabe asked, leaning his chin on his hand. "Did Nate have some news to share? Has Leo attacked anyone?"

Nick hesitated, then dove in. "Not, it's not that. I found out something pretty crazy yesterday. There's this kid named Ricky who's our age... and he's a medium, like me."

"Really?" Gabe raised an eyebrow. "And how did you find out about him?"

"Here's where it gets weird," Nick continued, running a hand through his hair. "I accidentally entered his mind while he was channeling. Somehow, we both figured out we were mediums. We've agreed to meet up tomorrow, face-to-face."

"Wow, that's... unexpected." Gabe frowned slightly, picking at his fries.

"Are you okay?" Nick asked, concern lining his voice.

"Umm....truthfully?" Gabe admitted, avoiding Nick's eyes. "I guess I'm just... a little jealous."

"Jealous?" Nick blinked. "Why would you be jealous?"

"Because," Gabe sighed, "you have these amazing powers, and now you've found someone else who does, too. I can't help but worry that ... you'll dump me for someone who's more like you."

"Hey," Nick said softly, reaching across the table to take Gabe's hand. "You never, ever have any reason to be jealous or to worry. You are the love of my life, Gabe Griffin. Psychic or not, nobody could ever come between us. Never. I mean it."

Gabe looked at him, searching his eyes for sincerity. "Really?"

"Really, truly, really," Nick affirmed, giving Gabe's hand a squeeze. "You're the person I want by my side, no matter what."

"Okay," Gabe whispered, a small smile appearing on his face. "I just needed to hear it, I guess."

"I realize I don't say it enough, but I love you more than anything," Nick said, placing one hand on his chest.

"Me too," Gabe said, finally taking a bite of his burger. "So, what do you think this meeting with Ricky will be like?"

"Who knows?" Nick shrugged. "But hey, why don't you come with me? I'd love for you to meet him too."

Gabe hesitated before shaking his head. "Nah, I'll sit this one out. I'll let you two talk about psychic stuff. But I'll be rooting for you from the sidelines. So, will Ricky be joining you and the other psychics to fight Leo?"

"Dammit!" said Nick.

Gabe widened his eyes. "What is it?"

"I forgot to tell Nate about Ricky. When we were chatting, I told Ricky about what was going on with this Leo business and he said he'd assist in any way possible. That's the purpose of our meeting in person, to tell him about everything that's been going on. I'll have to tell Nate later on at the lodge and see what he thinks." Nick ran his fingers through his hair. "I dunno how much Ricky can help, though. He's a completely different type of medium than me."

"Different? How so?"

"You know how I can see ghosts that haven't crossed over? Ricky, on the other hand, only can see ghosts who have already crossed over. But I don't think he sees them like I do in the real world. He both sees them and communicates with them in his mind. But maybe his connection to the other side can help us in some way. I'll have to mention it to the psychics."

Gabe considered this for a long moment. "Huh. Um... Do you think he could contact my sister?"

"That's a good question. I recall him saying that he has little control over it, over who comes through. I can ask him for you. Perhaps it's possible."

"Thanks, Nick. That would make me very happy."

CHAPTER NINE

A BLOOD-CURDLING SCREAM PIERCED THE STILLNESS of the night, shattering Nick's restless slumber. His heart thundered in his chest as he flung off the covers and raced to his sister's room, adrenaline surging through his veins.

Was Leo attacking his family?

He burst through the door to find Missy cowering in a corner, her eyes bulging and wild with fear as she gazed at an invisible horror.

"Missy!" their mother's panicked voice echoed in the air as she pushed past Nick to wrap her trembling daughter in a protective embrace.

"Mom! There's someone in my room!" Missy sobbed, burying her face in her mother's shoulder. "And her face is all bloody."

Nick's eyes roamed the room until they landed on the ghostly figure of an old woman by the dresser. She looked as though she'd been in a serious accident.

"Shh, it's okay," his mother whispered, trying to comfort her. Her eyes met Nick's, and Nick nodded, confirming his mother's suspicions. His mother's eyes widened in horror at the realization of what was occurring.

Nick's heart raced as he cautiously approached the old woman, now standing by Missy's bed. An icy chill crept up his spine, as he realized that his little sister was now just like him — able to see the spirits of the dead. The ghost's face bore deep wrinkles of sorrow, and its soulful eyes appeared to plead for help. The bloody gash on her forehead told the grim story of her end. Tears welled up in Nick's eyes as he whispered to the ghost, "I'm sorry. We can't help you now. Please come back later."

His heart shattered into a million pieces as he watched his sister whimper and cry, her innocent mind unable to comprehend what had just happened. He turned to his mother with a sense of urgency.

"Mom, we can't keep this from her any longer," he whispered, barely able to speak through the lump in his throat. "It's time. She needs to know the truth."

His mother nodded solemnly in agreement, tears welling up in her eyes. She cleared her throat. "Missy, sweetheart, there's something you need to know about your brother and about yourself." She cradled Missy's face gently, wiping away her tears with her thumbs. "The person that you just now observed in your room was not a person. It was a ghost. Nick also has the ability to perceive ghosts, just like you experienced tonight."

Missy's slight frame trembled as she looked up at Nick with wide, curious eyes. Her nose was red and her cheeks stained with tears. "Really?" she sniffled. "That scary lady ...she was a ghost?"

Nick knelt down beside her, his hand reaching out to take hers. "Yes, she was," he confirmed softly. "And apparently, it looks like you can see them just like I can."

Nick had always believed it was only the men in their family who had the gift of seeing spirits because that was what his Uncle Mitch had told him. But apparently, they were mistaken. Goosebumps rose on his arms as he realized the implications — that they shared a unique and powerful ability possibly passed down through generations. The truth was slowly unraveling before Nick's eyes as he gazed into hers, and he couldn't help but feel a sense of wonder and excitement at this newfound connection between them. He was fortunate in that his first encounter with a spirit did not happen until he turned 16, but Missy, on the other hand, was still a child at 13. Much too young to deal with any of this.

"But I don't want to see them!" she cried. Her body trembled in his mother's arms. "And I don't want them coming into my room!"

"I know you don't," said her mother soothingly. "But there are some things in this life that we don't have control over." She sighed. "But don't worry. Nick will explain everything to you. It's not as scary as it may seem. He'll help you through this."

Missy looked up at her mother with wide eyes. "Can you and Dad see them too?" Her voice brimmed with eager curiosity.

Their mother shook her head. "No, just you and your brother."

"Um... actually, that's not entirely true," Nick's father interjected, clearing his throat awkwardly before continuing. He glanced at Nick and Liz. "I can see them too. I've always been able to." His words hung in the air, dropping like an unexpected weight and causing a tense silence to settle over the room.

Nick's mother's jaw dropped in shock, her eyes widening as they darted back and forth between her husband and son. "You see spirits, John? And you never thought to mention it?" she exclaimed, her voice rising in disbelief. "How could you keep something like this from me for so long?"

Tension filled the room as Nick's father shifted uncomfortably, avoiding his wife's gaze. Nick stood there in stunned silence, shocked that his father, after all this time, had finally told his mother the truth. Nick was the only other person in the world who knew his father's secret.

"It's complicated," Nick's father tried to explain, his tone strained. "I didn't want to scare you or put our family at risk. But now that Missy has also inherited this ability, I decided it was time for me to be honest."

Anger and hurt flashed across his wife's face as she struggled to process this revelation.

Nick stood frozen, caught between guilt for keeping it hidden for so long from his mother and relief that his father had finally told the truth. Unspoken emotions hung heavy in the air as they all grappled with the magnitude of what had been hidden from them.

His mother's voice trembled with a mixture of shock, confusion, and a hint of betrayal. "I never once suspected that you... were like this. That you could do this. There were no indications."

"I never engaged with them... the ghosts," John said, his voice wavering. "I always pretended not to see them, so they would leave me alone. I figured it would be for the best not to tell anyone."

"John, why on earth did you believe it would be for the best?" His mother's eyebrows furrowed in concern as she struggled to understand. "To not tell me something as important as that?"

"Because of what happened with my brother," John whispered. "You remember the dinner with your parents, don't you? How you reacted after you found out about Mitch — how you treated him after that?"

"That's not fair!" His mother's voice rose with emotion, her eyes brimming with tears as she spoke. "I didn't understand any of it. I didn't know it was real. You could have sat me down and explained it all to me." She reached for a tissue from the top of Missy's dresser and dabbed at her tears before looking back at John with a pained expression. "And it was almost 20 years ago."

"Mom, Dad, can we talk about this later?" Nick interjected, seeing the escalating tension between his parents. Their lives had just taken a sharp turn, and they needed to focus on helping Missy understand her new reality.

"Uncle Mitch could see them, too?" asked Missy.

Nick sat on the bed next to his sister and took hold of her hand. "Uh-huh. He was the one who first taught me about them when I was scared and confused, just like you."

His parents grew silent, embarrassment evident in their expressions. "Missy," Nick continued. "There are others out there like us, people who can see and help ghosts," Nick explained, trying to keep his voice steady. "We're here to help them find peace." He fought the urge to give his father a dirty look, but resisted it.

"Will they always be this scary?" Missy asked, her bottom lip still trembling.

"Sometimes," Nick admitted, unwilling to sugarcoat the truth. "But most of the time, they're just confused. They don't remember what happened to them. So they come to us for help. But as you help them and communicate with them, they start to look more and more like regular people. You don't have to face this alone, Missy. We have each other. I'll teach you everything I can. I'm sure my friend Katrina will help too."

"That weird new age lady?"

Nick laughed. "The one and only. She's an expert in this stuff."

"Okay," Missy whispered, clinging to Nick's hand as if it were a lifeline. "Can I ignore them like Daddy?"

Nick took a deep breath before responding, avoiding his father's gaze. "That is one option, yes. It's probably best for the time being if you pretend you can't see them. We'll talk about this a lot more tomorrow. The lady is gone now, so you can get back to sleep."

"I can't believe this is happening," their mother said, her eyes glistening with unshed tears. She threw both hands into the air. "Now I have to worry about both my children."

"We'll be fine," Nick and Missy declared in unison, acknowledging that the world they had once known had changed forever.

Nick slipped out of Missy's room and pulled his phone from his pocket, scrolling through the contacts until he found Katrina's number. He hesitated for a moment before pressing the call button, worrying about how she would react to the news.

"Nicholas?" Katrina's voice was groggy on the other end of the line, clearly woken from sleep.

"Katrina, I'm sorry for calling so late, but it's about my sister, Missy," he said urgently, glancing over his shoulder to make sure no one was listening. "Apparently she... she has developed the ability to see ghosts."

"Oh no," Katrina muttered under her breath. "This could not have come at a worse time. You're sure of this?"

"Positive. There was a ghost of a woman in her bedroom and Missy screamed, believing it was an intruder."

There was a quiet lull in the conversation, heavy with unspoken fear. "You must get her out of town, Nick, as soon as possible. If Leo discovers her abilities..."

A shiver ran down Nick's spine at the thought of the possible dangers his sister could face. He interrupted, rubbing a hand through his curly hair in frustration. "That's already crossed my mind. I'll talk to my family first thing in the morning and try to convince them to leave town." The weight of responsibility sat heavily on his shoulders as he considered the safety of his sister. "Or do you think the psychics might help her?"

"Perhaps they can guide her when this is over," Katrina replied hesitantly. "But right now, protecting her is the most important thing, and she needs to be somewhere that is not Gallowspine Mountains. Get your family somewhere safe, Nicholas."

"I will," Nick agreed. "Thanks, Katrina."

"Stay safe," she whispered before hanging up.

Nick heard whispers coming from downstairs. Apparently, nobody had gone back to bed. Nick let out a deep sigh as he returned to the living room where his family waited, their faces etched with concern. "I realize you said earlier that you wanted to stay in your own house, but that's no longer an option. You must leave town," he announced, his voice heavy with the weight of their new reality. "Missy isn't safe here. None of you are."

His father frowned, his jaw set in determination. "Maybe I can stay and help. We can get your mother and sister somewhere safe. I'm happy to lend a hand in any way possible."

"Absolutely not," Nick countered firmly, remembering the warning from the creepy entity he'd encountered a couple of months back. "Dad, you're not meant to play a role in this upcoming battle. You need to stay safe so you can mentor Missy if... if anything happens to me."

"Nick!" his mother gasped, her eyes wide with fear. "Don't even say that!"

"Mom, it's a possibility we have to face," he insisted, his eyes welling with tears at the idea of leaving them. "I need you two to focus on keeping Missy safe."

"Will staying with the psychics be enough to protect you?" his father asked, his voice trembling.

"I hope so," Nick admitted, swallowing hard. "It's our best chance."

"Okay," his mother whispered, her hand clutching her husband's tightly as she nodded in agreement. "We'll leave town in the morning. We'll go to — "

"No," said Nick, shaking his head. "Don't tell me where you're going. Who knows whether Leo can read thoughts? I don't want to take any chances. The less I know about where you'll be, the better."

"Understood," she said. "But promise me, Nick. Promise me you'll do whatever it takes to stay alive."

He squeezed her hand tightly. "I will," he choked out, the burden of their survival weighing heavily on his shoulders.

"What, what battle? Missy asked.

"A battle against something that's too scary for words. I'll tell you all about it when it's over."

"But you'll be okay, right?" Missy added softly, her eyes shining.

"Missy, I swear on my life," Nick replied, pulling her into a tight embrace. "I will do everything I can to come back to you and Mom and Dad."

"Alright," Missy whispered, holding onto him as if he were her anchor in the storm that raged around them.

"Okay," Nick agreed, clinging to the hope that they would all make it through this nightmare together.

CHAPTER TEN

A GENTLE BREEZE RUSTLED THROUGH THE TREES, stirring up a whirlwind of crimson and gold leaves in the small park where Nick stood. He squinted up at the sky, noting the overcast clouds that seemed to be a physical manifestation of the town's collective unease. It had been a week since the psychics arrived, and still, there was no sign of Leo. The uncertainty gnawed at everyone, leaving them in a perpetual state of tension.

"Focus, Nick," urged Vivian, her voice firm yet patient. She was the psychic who'd been working with him, helping him to hone his abilities.

"Right, sorry." Nick shook off his lingering thoughts and took a deep breath, centering himself. He needed to concentrate on his training. As he closed his eyes, an image of the tarot card he'd chosen earlier at the lodge flashed before his mind's eye — The Hanged Man.

"Visualize the card, Nick," instructed Vivian. "Let its energy flow through you." Her voice was calm and soothing as it guided him through the exercise.

As Nick sweated profusely under the blistering sun, he

tried desperately to focus on the card in front of him. A pesky fly broke his concentration, buzzing around his head, and he swatted at it with annoyance. "Can't I do this in air-conditioning?" he grumbled. It was unseasonably warm today and he'd overdressed, thinking it would be much cooler.

Despite the distractions, his mind was sharper than a freshly honed sword, thanks to the perfect combination of meditation and caffeine, and he controlled his visions like a master puppeteer. He could practically see them in 3D, with surround sound and special effects. And unlike before, when they would just pop up randomly and freak him out, now he was able to manipulate their intensity like a master DJ at a rave, allowing him to explore them without fear or anxiety.

But unfortunately, even with all this newfound mental clarity, Nick's visions were as unhelpful as a Magic 8 Ball. No matter how hard he concentrated or forced himself into a meditative state, there was no sign of Leo or his nefarious plans. For now, his visions told him nothing of import. Maybe he needed to switch to decaf.

But now, Nick couldn't help but wish he could use his powers to conjure up some ice-cold lemonade.

"Right, right," Nick muttered, snapping himself back to the task at hand, trying to tap into the energy of the Hanged Man card. He felt his body relax, while his mind became sharper and more focused. Visions flickered past his inner sight like a reel of film, each one more vivid than the last.

Suddenly, a cool breeze rustled through the trees, carrying Vivian's soothing voice to Nick's ears. "Good, Nick. You're doing great," praised Vivian. Her gentle touch on his shoulder, encouraged him to go deeper. The scent of pine and wet earth filled his nostrils, grounding him in the present moment. "Now, remember what we discussed about interpreting the cards? Use your instincts and allow yourself to understand the deeper meaning."

"Alright," Nick murmured, his brow furrowed in concentration as he sank further into the vision, the sun warm on his skin. The taste of sacrifice and surrender lingered on his tongue, reminding him to let go and see things from a different perspective — that sometimes you have to go with the flow and hang upside down if you want to succeed in life.

Nick understood he needed to embrace these qualities if he was going to succeed in his battle against Leo. He intuitively tapped into the energy of the scene and let it wash over him. A distant bird call broke through his musings, adding a bit of whimsy to the whole situation...until Vivian interrupted his thoughts with a whisper. He opened his eyes to see Vivian nodding at him with approval. With newfound understanding, Nick confidently shared his interpretation with Vivian.

"Very well done," commended Vivian as Nick opened his eyes. "I think you're ready for the next step."

"Which is?" asked Nick, curiosity piqued.

Vivian's expression turned serious, her voice tinged with reverence. "Working with tarot alongside your visions can be an incredibly potent combination," she explained. The weight of her words hung in the air, and Nick felt a tingle of excitement run through him.

He nonchalantly ran his fingers through his unruly hair as he replied, "Oh, I've been using tarot and my visions since the very beginning. My Uncle Mitch first taught me how to use it." A sly smile played at his lips. "It's given me an edge in solving quite a few ghostly mysteries along the way. In fact, most of my visions have occurred during a reading. Of course, then I was unable to control the visions — they'd come willy-nilly."

Vivian's serious expression faltered, replaced with surprise as she realized Nick had been one step ahead of her all along.

The sharp, shrill ring of Nick's cellphone suddenly shattered the peaceful silence. He shot an apologetic glance at Vivian before reaching into his pocket to retrieve the device. The screen lit up with his mother's name, and he let out a sigh as he answered. He held up an index finger to Vivian. "It's my mom."

"Hey, Mom," he greeted, trying to conceal the impatience that crept into his tone. His fingers nervously tapped against the phone as he waited for her response.

"Hi, honey," her voice sounded through the receiver, a mix of casual tones and underlying urgency. "I just got off the phone with Bree, Ryan's mom," she said, her tone casual but with a hint of urgency. "Remember, I told you about my friend's son reporting strange things in his room — strange disturbances and things moving around on their own."

"Oh right, Ryan." The name fell from his lips with a sense of unease, as if it carried its own weight.

"Yes. So I spoke with Bree and she agreed to have you stop by their house and check things out."

There was a silence. "What did you tell her?"

"I told her about your...special abilities. She requested you come by tomorrow morning at 10:00 am to assess the situation and potentially offer your help."

"Sure, I can do that," agreed Nick, already wondering what was causing the mysterious activity. Nick's mind raced, wondering what kind of situation he would find in Ryan's bedroom. Hopefully, it would be nothing but Ryan seeking attention. "But mom, what exactly did you tell Ryan's mom? About me, I mean."

"I explained that you've been working with some gifted individuals and have developed certain people skills that might be useful in this situation," she reassured him. "But I didn't go into too much detail. I got the impression that she thought I was talking about youth counseling or something similar and I didn't bother to correct her. I'm not sure how she'd react if I told her my son can communicate with the dead." She chuckled into the phone.

Nick let out a sigh of relief as he thanked his mother for not revealing the full extent of his psychic ability and his real reason for coming over to check things out. His heart raced with anticipation for what was to come. "I'll let you know how it goes."

"Good luck, honey. I'm positive you'll do your best," she encouraged, her voice warm and supportive.

"By the way, what's the timing looking like for leaving? When are you all hitting the road?" Nick asked, trying to sound casual despite the gnawing anxiety about the whole situation.

"We're just about ready, honey. The car's nearly packed. We hope to leave within the next hour," his mother replied, her tone light but rushed.

Nick nodded to himself, a frown creasing his brow. "That's good," he murmured.

His mother continued, oblivious to his growing tension, "And we'll be heading to —"

"Mom, don't," Nick interrupted sharply, his voice a mixture of fear and resolve. "Remember, I don't want to know where you're going."

There was a pause on the line, a moment of silence that was almost palpable. "Of course. I forgot. Oh, this is all so annoying." Understanding dawned in her voice, heavy and a little weary. "But, I understand, darling. You're right. It's better if we don't tell you."

Nick sighed, a mix of relief and lingering anxiety washing over him. "Just text me when you're safe. But keep it vague."

"We will. And don't worry, we'll be careful," she assured him.

"Thanks, Mom. And tell Dad to take it easy on the road, okay?"

"I will. Love you, Nick."

"Love you too, Mom." Nick ended the call, the weight of the conversation settling around him.

"Everything alright?" asked Vivian, concern etching her brow.

"Ryan's mom wants me to check out some disturbances at their house tomorrow morning," explained Nick. "Things moving around on their own. My mom is afraid that it's poltergeist activity."

Vivian's brow furrowed as she contemplated Nick's plan. "It might be a clever trap set by Leo, or perhaps something else entirely," she cautioned, her tone grave and serious. "Just remember, whatever happens, you are not to cross over any ghosts, under any circumstances. It's far too dangerous with Leo still at large, especially with him targeting you. It's best to not even communicate or acknowledge them, if possible."

Nick's excitement and nervousness mingled as he agreed. "I won't. I promise. I just hope it's nothing too serious. If it is a ghost, I would dread having to explain to Ryan what's going on. He's pretty much a dick most of the time."

She raised her eyebrows. "And who is this Ryan person again?"

"He's the kid who claims there are strange occurrences happening in his room. We go to school together."

"Ah, got it."

Nick's hands trembled as he spoke. "Truth be told, I'm kind of nervous about going there, Vivian. What if it's not just a simple ghost haunting this place, but one of Leo's twisted minions? Or worse, what if it's actually Leo himself — waiting for me? It'd be like walking into a death trap."

Vivian gave him an encouraging smile and placed a reassuring hand on his shoulder, but even her touch couldn't calm the knot in his stomach. The thought of facing his new enemy overwhelmed him.

"You've got this, Nick," she said firmly. "You've come a long way and you're stronger than you think. Trust in yourself and your instincts, and you'll get through anything. Also remember that if you run into trouble, we're only a call away. We'll come as quickly as we can. You never need to face anything alone."

Nick's stomach churned with nerves, but he nodded, grateful for her words of encouragement. "Thanks, Vivian," he whispered, drawing comfort from her words as they echoed in his mind.

Nick knew she was right. He had to trust himself and his abilities. Just then, his thoughts drifted to his little sister and the ghost she saw last night. He'd promised his mom that he would keep Missy's psychic abilities a secret from everyone — even from the psychics — and he intended to honor that promise. The image of his sister, wide-eyed and pale after seeing a ghost the night before, filled Nick with a sense of unease. This situation was already scary enough as it was, and he couldn't bear the thought of adding any more worry onto his family's plate. Nick hoped she'd be okay and couldn't help but be concerned for her. He couldn't bear the thought of something happening to her if she had to face a malevolent ghost or one of Leo's minions head-on, by herself.

So for now, Nick kept quiet about Missy's newfound abilities and focused on the task at hand; saving Ryan's house from any spirits in their midst.

CHAPTER ELEVEN

NICK'S FINGERS DANCED RHYTHMICALLY ON THE keyboard as the soft glow of his computer screen illuminated the dimly lit room. Despite the evening sun having long since dipped below the horizon, Nick remained engrossed in a world of online forums and research articles. He should call it a night and get some rest, but something about the electric hum of the computer and the seemingly endless wealth of knowledge at his fingertips kept him tethered to the desk.

The sudden, shrill ring of his cellphone sliced through the silence like a knife. Nick jumped in his seat as he glanced over at the screen, brow furrowing when he saw Gabe's name flashing brightly against the darkness. That was odd. Gabe never called him; he was more of a texter. Something must be wrong.

"Hey, man," Nick said cautiously, holding the phone tight to his ear. "What's up?"

"Nick!" Gabe's voice cracked with panic. "You gotta to help me! I think... I think someone or something attacked me! A gargoyle almost crushed me."

"A what?" Nick instinctively shot up from his chair, adrenaline surging through his veins.. "What the hell happened? Are you hurt?"

"Hurt? Physically, no. But mentally, man, I'm freaking out!" Gabe's words poured out in a frantic rush. "I went to the state building earlier to sign up for that part-time job, remember? And before I even made it inside, a freaking gargoyle statue fell from the roof and almost crushed me! And the same thing happened when I left the building! I was walking down the outside stairs and smash! Another gargoyle statue fell from the building and crashed right next to me. It's like someone's trying to kill me or something! I mean, that can't be a coincidence, right?" Gabe's voice cracked with terror as he recounted the harrowing experience.

Nick's blood ran cold at Gabe's revelation, an over-whelming sense of dread settling in his stomach. "Jesus, Gabe...Did anyone else see it happen? Are you sure you're not hurt?"

"No, luckily I didn't get hurt, but that's not even the worst part!" Gabe continued, his voice trembling. "I'm at home now, and suddenly there are knives flying at me from out of nowhere! I've had to dodge them like three times already!"

"Knives?" Nick repeated, his concern deepening as he tried to wrap his head around what was happening. "Gabe, that's... That doesn't make sense. Are you sure you're not just seeing things?"

"Seeing things?!" Gabe snapped, clearly offended by the suggestion. "This coming from the man who sees ghosts? No, this is *not* a figment of my imagination! It's all too real! And on top of everything else, I saw that kid again — Leo! He was wearing that red baseball cap like last time and was standing outside my house, watching me with those cold, dead eyes of his." The sheer terror in Gabe's voice sent chills down Nick's spine.

"Leo?" Nick's blood ran cold at the mention of the mysterious demon-in-a-boy's-body they'd encountered before. The demon. It seemed it was now targeting Gabe. A lump of dread settled into Nick's stomach.

Nick's voice trembled with barely contained panic as he spoke, the sound of his own words ringing hollow in his ears. "Gabe, listen to me," he commanded, his tone firm and urgent despite the fear and confusion raging inside him. His stomach churned and twisted violently. "I'm on my way. Just hold on and, for God's sake, steer clear of those... knives, or whatever they are. I'll be there as soon as possible. I swear I won't let anything happen to you."

Gabe responded with desperation and terror. "Please, Nick," he begged, his voice quavering uncontrollably. "Hurry. I can't take much more of this. My parents aren't here and I'm here all alone, trapped in this nightmare. Let me tell you, this is a whole new level of terrifying"

"Stay strong, babe," Nick encouraged him before ending the call. He snatched his jacket and keys from the nearby hook and bolted out the door, his mind racing a mile a minute.

As he sped through the empty streets toward Gabe's house, a growing sense of dread clawed at his insides. Why was the demon now targeting Gabe? What could it possibly want with him? Nick knew the answer; the demon was targeting Gabe to get to Nick. Nate had warned him this might happen.

Nick skidded to a halt outside Gabe's house, gravel crunching beneath the tires as he threw the car into park and sprinted toward the front door. It was unlocked, and he barged in without a moment's hesitation.

"Gabe!" he shouted, eyes darting around the darkened living room for any sign of his friend. "Where are you?"

"Upstairs!" came Gabe's panicked response, followed by a loud crash and what sounded like a muffled curse.

Nick took the stairs two at a time, heart hammering against his ribs as he reached the top and flung open Gabe's bedroom door. His boyfriend looked like a wreck — hair disheveled, clothes torn, and shaking like a leaf as he clung to the headboard of his bed for dear life.

"Nick," Gabe choked out, visibly relieved to see him. "Thank God you're here."

He pulled Gabe into a tight hug. Gabe buried his face in Nick's neck and held him close. Gabe trembled in Nick's arms.

"Are you okay?" Nick asked urgently, scanning the room for any sign of the knives Gabe had mentioned. "Did anything else happen while I was on my way?"

"More knives," Gabe admitted, shuddering at the memory. "I barely avoided them. But they just... disappeared after that and haven't been back. I went to hide in the closet. But Nick, I swear, it was not my imagination."

Nick's voice was low and strained as he muttered under his breath, the muscles in his jaw tight with anger and fear. "Damn it," he hissed, "this has gone far enough." He could feel the coiling tension in his gut, a sense of dread that threatened to suffocate him. "That frigging demon is targeting you, Gabe. I was afraid this would happen." An icy shiver ran down his spine as he spoke, the dangerous reality of their situation hitting him like a ton of bricks.

Gabe looked back at him, his eyes wide with alarm. "What do you mean?" he asked, his voice shaking.

"I mean, it's not safe for you here anymore," Nick replied, his tone urgent and serious. "You need to get out of town until this is all over. I mean it. There is no other option. No more avoiding the inevitable."

Gabe's brow creased, as though his mind were racing, trying to comprehend the gravity of the situation. "But what about my parents?"

Nick softened his expression. "We'll think of something," he promised. "But right now, your safety is the most important thing. Trust me on this. And we need to do it sooner rather than later."

Gabe's shoulders slumped. "I know you're right."

"Your parents aren't home right now, right?" Nick asked, remembering Gabe mentioning that they'd be away for the evening. "We can figure something out, but we need to act fast. The longer you stay here, the more danger you'll be in. Tonight, I want you to stay with the psychics at the lodge. They'll be able to protect you there. But first thing tomorrow, you gotta somehow convince your parents to leave town — or at least let you leave town on your own."

"Okay," Gabe agreed hesitantly, his fear momentarily overshadowed by determination. "Let's do this. I need to get away from whatever this thing wants with me. But first, I need your help to pack a bag. My hands are shaking too much."

"Of course," Nick nodded, setting aside his own fears for the moment as he focused on helping his boyfriend. He cupped Gabe's face with his hands and kissed him. "It'll be okay. Let's just keep moving."

Together, they hastily stuffed clothes, toiletries, and other essentials into a duffel bag. As the weight of the situation settled in, Nick couldn't help but worry about what lay ahead.

Bringing Gabe to the lodge was only a temporary solution, and that Gabe would need to get far away from here as soon as possible. But for now, all that mattered was keeping him safe tonight — at any cost.

With a feeling of finality, Gabe pulled the zipper closed on the duffel bag, his fingers fidgeting nervously around the metal. He glanced at Nick with uncertain eyes, silently asking for reassurance. In response, Nick could see the wheels turning in his friend's mind.

"Actually," Gabe began, his voice slightly steadier than before, "I talked to my parents earlier about maybe going to stay with my grandma for a little while, just in case. Surprisingly, they said it was fine. I think that might be a good, safe place for me to go."

Nick let out a small sigh of relief, glad that there was already an option in place. Gabe's grandmother lived in a small town several hours away — far enough that it would hopefully throw the demon off their trail, but close enough that they could still keep in touch and work on a plan.

"Great idea," he agreed, slinging the bag over his shoulder. "See if you can convince them to let you go as soon as tomorrow. But for tonight, we'll stay together at the lodge. The psychics there can add some extra protections around you, just in case. One of them is a witch, you know. Quite powerful, from what I understand."

"Really?" Gabe asked, his eyes widening in surprise.

"Yep," Nick replied, trying to inject some confidence into his tone. "Her name's Eliza. She's been helping me with all this demon stuff. She's the one that was staying with us to help protect my family before they left town. I'm sure she'll be able to do something for you, too."

"Okay," Gabe said, his expression still tinged with apprehension. "Let's go then."

As they descended the stairs, Nick couldn't help but notice how different Gabe's house felt now. What had once been a warm, welcoming space filled with laughter and memories now seemed tainted by the sinister presence that had invaded their lives. He was aware that, even after they dealt with the demon, things would never quite be the same.

Gabe stood hesitantly at the front door, his hand hovering over the doorknob. "Hey, uh, Nick?" he said, his voice shaky with fear. "What if this doesn't work? What if that thing just keeps coming after me?"

Nick's expression hardened as he stepped forward and took Gabe's hand in his own. Their fingers intertwined, a comforting warmth spreading between them. Bringing their joined hands up to his lips, Nick kissed the back of Gabe's hand tenderly. "Then we'll come up with another plan," he declared firmly. "We won't rest until you're safe, I promise."

A small smile tugged at the corner of Gabe's lips as he looked into Nick's unwavering gaze. "Thanks," he murmured gratefully. "I'm glad you're here with me through all of this."

"Me too, man," Nick said, returning the smile as they stepped outside and locked the door behind them.

THE SUN HAD DIPPED below the horizon by the time they reached the lodge, casting eerie shadows across the overgrown yard as they approached the old building.

As they entered the dimly lit foyer, the scent of incense greeted them, mingling with the faint mustiness that clung to every corner of the ancient building. A motley assortment of candles flickered on various surfaces, casting a warm, if somewhat unstable, glow over the scene.

"Nick!" called a familiar voice from the shadows, and Helena emerged, her wizened face creased into a welcoming grin. "And you must be Gabe," she added, turning her attention to the nervous young man beside him. "We've been expecting you."

"Expecting me?" Gabe stammered, taken aback. "How did you know I was coming?"

"Word travels fast in our circles," Helena replied cryptically, her eyes twinkling with amusement. "But in all seriousness, Nick texted us and told us you'd be arriving. Now, let's get started, shall we?"

She led them down a narrow hallway lined with shelves crammed full of books and strange artifacts, the floorboards creaking ominously beneath their feet. Gabe stared wide-eyed at the bizarre assortment of items, his curiosity momentarily overpowering his fear.

"What's all this stuff?" he asked, gesturing towards an especially grotesque-looking mask that seemed to leer at him from its perch on the wall.

"Tools of the trade," Helena answered simply, pushing open a door at the end of the hall and ushering them inside. "It's all stuff we've brought with us."

The room they entered was small and cluttered, filled with even more oddities than the hallway. A large wooden table dominated the space, covered in a frayed cloth embroidered with intricate symbols. Several other people sat around it, their faces serious and focused as they looked up at the newcomers.

"Everyone," Helena announced, "this is Gabe. He's the one for whom we've been preparing. He'll be spending the night with us here at the lodge."

"Hi," Gabe mumbled, looking suddenly very vulnerable under the scrutiny of so many strangers.

Nick, with a firm grip on Gabe's hand, eagerly led the way. His excitement was palpable and contagious. "Come on," he urged, his voice brimming with enthusiasm. "Let me show you where you'll be staying."

Helena hesitated, her eyes flickering with unease. "Um... Nick?" she said tentatively.

Nick stopped in his tracks and turned back to face Helena, his expression curious. "What is it?" he asked.

"Your mother called," Helena began slowly. "She said that you and Gabe are not to share the same bedroom."

Nick and Gabe exchanged a knowing look before bursting into laughter. "That's my mom for you," Nick chuckled, shaking his head in amusement. Not that they would allow this rule to put a damper on their plans or their excitement for the evening ahead.

CHAPTER TWELVE

THE RAIN PATTERED SOFTLY ON THE WINDOWPANE, creating a soothing rhythm that accompanied the soft murmur of conversations inside the cozy cafe. Steam curled upward from two steaming cappuccinos on the small table near the back, where Nick and Ricky sat, their faces mirrored in the foggy glass.

"Alright, so let me get this straight," said Ricky, rubbing his temples as he tried to absorb the vast amount of information Nick had just shared. His eyes were wide with disbelief, and he took an absent-minded sip from his coffee. "This demon, Leo, is called The Dark One, and he's capturing souls and killing psychics?"

"Exactly," confirmed Nick, leaning forward earnestly, his hands wrapped around his cup for warmth. "And I'm supposed to be The Light One, the one who's destined to stop him. Or at least, that's what they tell me."

"Wow, man, that's... intense," Ricky breathed, his eyebrows knitting together with concern. "I have sensed recently that something was amiss with the spirit world, but

I never would have guessed it was at this level. And you've been training with these European psychics at a resort in the Gallowspine Mountains to prepare for all this?"

Nick nodded, his face serious. "They're teaching me how to harness my abilities, to protect myself and others from Leo's dark forces. They tell me there's going to be a battle between me and him soon, but nobody knows when or where it'll happen. We just have to be ready."

Ricky stared at his new friend, perhaps seeing the weight of responsibility that now rested on Nick's shoulders. He shook his head in amazement, his earlier skepticism giving way to awe. "I can't believe this is happening to you, dude. But I sense that if anyone can handle it, it's you. Given that you entered my meditations though we had never met, I'd venture to say that you're a lot more powerful than you think you are. It certainly isn't something I could do."

"Thanks, man," Nick replied, a hint of a smile flickering across his face. "But I didn't come here to talk about me. I need your help."

"Sure, anything for you," Ricky said, his voice filled with determination.

"Ricky, you're the only one I know who can communicate with those who have crossed over," Nick began, his voice low and urgent. "Can you please try to get in touch with my Uncle Mitch? There's something important I need to find out from him. I need to know if he crossed over when he passed, or if Leo captured him before he had the chance." His voice was urgent, a mix of fear and desperation driving him to seek answers from beyond. "I also want to find out if Leo was behind his death."

"Wow, that's intense, man," Ricky said. "Of course I'll

help you. Be warned, though, I can't guarantee that I'll be able to connect with a specific person. It's more of a hit-or-miss kind of thing. But I'm willing to try." He took a sip of his coffee before closing his eyes and focusing on the task at hand. "Let me just clear my mind and tune into the spiritual realm. What's the full name of the person you're trying to reach?"

"Mitchell Michelson."

As Ricky concentrated, Nick watched his new friend intently, noting how Ricky's brow furrowed as he reached out to the other side. The cafe seemed to fade away, its background noises becoming distant and unimportant as all of Nick's attention focused on Ricky's efforts.

"Anything?" Nick asked after a few minutes, trying to keep the impatience out of his voice.

Ricky opened his eyes, shaking his head in frustration. "I'm sorry, Nick. I tried, but I just can't reach him. Now that doesn't mean he's not there. Tuning in to a specific person can be quite unpredictable. But I noticed that something's off... there's a major disturbance on the other side. It's like everything's out of balance. I've felt it a lot recently."

"Leo," Nick muttered darkly, clenching his fists around his cup. "It has to be him. He's disrupting the natural order of things, probably because there aren't enough souls crossing over."

"Perhaps," Ricky agreed, his expression grave. "I've noticed that the veil separating our world from the spirit realm is getting thinner, and that can't be good for any of us."

Nick sighed, sensing a heaviness settle on his chest as he considered the implications of this fresh development.

"Thanks for trying, Ricky," he said quietly, genuinely grateful for his friend's efforts. "I'm aware this isn't your fight, but I appreciate you being here for me."

"Hey, we're all in this together, man," Ricky replied with a small grin, reaching across the table to pat Nick reassuringly on the arm. "Whatever I can do to help, just let me know."

"Thank you," Nick repeated.

Nick gazed through the rain-streaked window of the cafe, watching people rush past under umbrellas and through puddles. He felt a strange sense of disconnection from the world outside, as if the events unfolding in his life had placed him on an entirely different plane of existence.

"Hey, Nick," Ricky said, pulling his attention back to their conversation. "I've been thinking about all this psychic stuff we've been dealing with, and I think there might be something I can do to help you out."

"Really?" Nick asked, intrigued. Ricky's abilities differed from his own — whereas Nick communicated with spirits before they crossed over, Ricky connected with them once they'd gone into the Light. Still, he was eager for any help that might bolster his chances against Leo.

"How about if we work together?" Ricky suggested, his eyes lighting up with excitement. "Like a team. I might not fight by your side or whatever, but I could try to gather information from spirits who've crossed over. Perhaps they possess some valuable information about this Leo character and what he's been up to."

Nick considered the offer but didn't want Ricky attracting Leo's attention. "Ricky, I appreciate the offer," Nick said, touched by his friend's willingness to step into the fray. "But it's too dangerous. I don't want to put you at risk. Besides, I already have support from the European psychics."

"Okay, okay," Ricky conceded, raising his hands defensively. "I get it. You don't want me tangling with the Dark One. But hey, if you ever need someone to chat with the dearly departed..."

"Thank you," Nick said sincerely, clasping Ricky's shoulder. "I'll keep that in mind. Now that I think about it, it might be helpful to ask the spirits who've crossed over if they've heard anything or know anything. From what we understand, Leo only interferes with mediums like me. But I'll check with the psychics to see what they say. But in the meantime, hold off until after I talk to them."

Ricky gave him a salute. "Will do, Captain."

As Ricky went to the counter to order another coffee, Nick pulled out his phone and dialed Katrina's number, hoping she might have some insight into the situation at hand. When her soothing voice came through the speaker, it was like a balm to his frayed nerves.

"Hey, Katrina," he began, "I just met up with Ricky, the medium I told you about. He tried to contact my Uncle Mitch, but was unable to reach him."

"Ah, I forgot about his abilities," Katrina replied gently. "That he can communicate with those who have already crossed over. Hmm... if your uncle is still in limbo, unable to communicate with either of you because he's under Leo's control, then it makes sense that he didn't come through. It's what we've both suspected. Let us hope that's not the case."

"I hope not," Nick said. "Oh, and Ricky also said he could sense a major disturbance on the other side, like the veil is getting thinner. I can't shake the feeling that Leo's behind it all, somehow."

"Sounds about right for our resident demon," Katrina

sighed. "It makes sense, given he's trying to disrupt the balance between life and death to further his own twisted goals."

"Exactly," Nick agreed, clenching his fist around the phone. "That's why I need to do a tarot reading to find out what he's been up to. I've tried at the lodge, but there were too many distractions. I've had visions, but they were only about mundane things — nothing about Leo's plans. Maybe I'll have better luck at my house, even if it might be creepy since my parents and sister left town. But almost every vision I've had while reading cards has been at home."

"Be careful, Nick," Katrina warned, her voice laced with concern. "You never know when or where Leo will strike next."

"Thanks, Katrina," he responded, taking a deep breath to steady himself. "I'll call you after the reading if anything comes up."

"Good luck," she said softly before hanging up.

As Nick pocketed his phone, a strange mix of fear and determination settled in his gut. Delving deeper into Leo's machinations was a dangerous game, but he wasn't about to sit idly by while the demon wreaked havoc on both the living and the dead. It was time to take action, to take the offensive.

"Hey, man," Ricky said as he returned to the table with a fresh cup of coffee to go. "You ready to head out?"

"Let's do it," Nick replied, forcing a smile onto his face for Ricky. "I'll walk you to your car."

Ricky nodded, his expression solemn, as they donned their jackets and stepped outside into the rain. As they made their way through the downpour, a shiver ran down his spine, knowing that this was only the beginning of the storm that was about to engulf his life.

"Ricky," Nick called out over the sound of raindrops pelting their umbrellas. "Be safe."

"Always, man," Ricky replied, and he fist-bumped Nick. "You too."

$\approx$

THE RAIN FELL in heavy droplets, their incessant tapping filling the air as Nick unlocked the door to his family's now empty home. The place had a strange aura of coldness and unfamiliarity. Each creak of the floorboards had him on edge, his heart pounding in his chest as if it was trying to escape.

"Okay, Nick," he muttered under his breath, steadying himself with a deep inhale. "You've done this before. You can do it again. Stop being such a wuss."

He made his way through the house, methodically flicking on lights as he went, chasing away the darkness that seemed intent on engulfing everything around him. When he reached his bedroom — the room he typically used for readings, he hesitated, his hand hovering over the light switch. This was where he usually experienced the strongest connection to his psychic abilities, but the thought of what he might uncover about Leo — the Dark One — sent chills racing down his spine.

"Focus," Nick commanded himself, flipping the switch and flooding the room with light. He closed the door behind him, wanting to keep the outside world at bay while he concentrated on his task. Setting up his reading table, he lit several candles to help focus his energy and turned off the overhead light. The warm glow from the candles cast dancing shadows on the walls.

"Alright," he said, rubbing his hands together briskly. "Let's see what you've been up to, Leo."

Nick began his reading, shuffling his deck of tarot cards with practiced ease. As he laid them out one by one, his brow furrowed in concentration. The images seemed to blur together, morphing into something twisted and dark. It was as if the demon's presence had tainted the very essence of Nick's cards. The most unsettling cards in the deck were the ones that appeared: The Tower, The Devil, 10 of Swords and 3 of Swords.

"Damn it," he muttered, aware of beads of sweat forming on his forehead. "Why isn't this working?"

He tried again, attempting to clear his mind and focus solely on the task at hand. But as hard as he tried, he couldn't shake the feeling that something wasn't right — like a presence lurking just beyond his line of sight. The situation proved unnerving, making it impossible for him to concentrate.

"Come on," he whispered, frustrated with himself. "You've got this."

As the minutes ticked by, Nick's frustration grew. He'd never struggled with a reading like this before, and it only added to his sense of powerlessness. The knowledge that Leo was out there wreaking havoc weighed heavily on his mind. He felt responsible, as if it was his duty to stop the Dark One before it became too late.

"Okay," he said, taking a calming breath. "One more try."

Nick's fingers trembled as he shuffled the tarot deck, his heart pounding in anticipation. A chill settled over the room, and an uneasy silence enveloped him. He couldn't shake off the feeling that something dreadful was about to happen, but he desperately needed to know Leo's plans.

"Show me what I need to see," he whispered to the cards, laying them out on the table. His eyes lingered on each card, searching for meaning, for answers. As he turned over the last card, a sudden flash of light blinded him, plunging him into another world.

He now stood in the town square, surrounded by pandemonium and destruction. The sky above was a swirling mass of inky blackness, lit up by sharp bolts of lightning that cut through the air like jagged blades. It was as if the very fabric of existence was tearing apart, signaling the impending doom of all things.

Enormous boulders hurtled from the heavens with a deafening crash, obliterating everything in their path. Buildings crumbled like sandcastles beneath the force of their impact, and desperate screams filled the air. Each deafening cry pierced through him, causing his heart to race and his blood to run cold. In a rapid succession, horrific images of death and destruction flashed before his eyes, each one more terrifying than the last. He felt as though he were drowning in a sea of chaos and devastation.

As the mayhem raged around them, Nick's eyes caught sight of Leo, standing tall and confident amidst the madness. A wicked smile played across his lips as he surveyed the destruction. His figure appeared almost ethereal, bathed in shadows, as if he were a creature from another realm. But he wasn't alone. Behind him, a horde of grotesque creatures shuffled forward, their moans and groans filling the air with a macabre symphony. At first glance, they appeared to be ghostly apparitions, but upon closer inspection, their rotting flesh and vacant eyes revealed them to be more akin to zombies than anything else — they were souls now fully under Leo's control.

The crackle of lightning and the howl of the wind filled

the air as Leo's maniacal laughter echoed through the stormy skies. Thunder rumbled in the distance as Leo, a towering figure with a menacing grin, now stood before Nick. The air crackled with energy, reflecting the mayhem unfolding around them. Nick's heart raced as he watched, muttering curses under his breath.

"Join us, Nick! Embrace the darkness!" Leo taunted, his voice booming like thunder. But Nick stood firm, clenching his fists in determination.

Never," Nick spat back, his voice trembling. And in the midst of it all, he noticed the familiar decorations and banners that could only mean one thing — this scene was occurring during the upcoming Founder's Day celebration. A surge of fear coursed through him as he realized the gravity of the situation and what was at stake.

The blinding light of the vision abruptly faded, leaving Nick disoriented and back in the dimly lit room. The searing pain that always accompanied his visions slammed into his skull like a sledgehammer, causing him to wince in agony. He reached up to rub his throbbing temples, trying to ease some of the discomfort. But the ache persisted, pulsing through his head with every beat of his heart.

"Ugh... these damn headaches..." he groaned, gritting his teeth against the pain. Despite the overwhelming urge to give in to the pain and drift off into unconsciousness, he knew there was no time to waste. Now that he'd glimpsed Leo's sinister plan, and it was now his responsibility to put an end to it. The urgency of the situation left no room for delay or hesitation. The relentless pounding in his head only fueled his determination to stop Leo's evil scheme from coming to fruition.

"Founder's Day..." Nick muttered, trying to piece together his thoughts as the pain subsided. "It's only a couple of days away. I've got to warn the others... I won't let you destroy our town, Leo."

His resolve hardened, Nick gathered the tarot cards with trembling hands. No matter how terrifying the vision had been, he would do everything in his power to prevent that apocalyptic scene from becoming a reality.

He had to.

CHAPTER THIRTEEN

Nick hesitated at the entrance of Ryan's house, his hand poised to knock on the door. The late afternoon sun cast long shadows across the front porch, and a chill breeze rustled the leaves of the nearby oak tree. He took a deep breath, inhaling the sweet scent of autumn, and then rapped sharply on the door. A moment later, it swung open to reveal Ryan's bemused expression.

"Hey, man," Nick said casually, as though he and Ryan were friends, which they were not. Or at least, not anymore. "I understand you've had some... disturbances?"

Ryan rolled his eyes, the exasperation clear on his face as he leaned against the wooden door frame. He let out a heavy sigh, his frustration clear in the way he slumped his shoulders. "I can't believe my mom had you come over here," he scoffed. "Like, what are you supposed to do? Counsel me? Be my shrink?" Sarcasm and annoyance laced his tone, as if he couldn't fathom why anyone would think talking to someone would solve his problems.

"You never know, I might be able to help," Nick said. "Can you tell me more about what's going on?"

His fingers raked through his disheveled hair in frustration. "I don't know what you think you can do about it," he
sighed, his voice laced with annoyance. "It's just...weird shit
happening in my room. Things getting moved around,
strange noises, whispering voices I can't explain." He shuddered. "Last week, a book flew straight at me from my desk
and scared the crap out of me," he added, crossing his arms
defensively over his chest. "So Michelson, why did you even
bother coming here?"

"Ah, I'm always looking for an excuse to drop by and see
my favorite troublemaker." Nick grinned, trying to keep the
conversation light.

"Whatever. Come in, I guess." Ryan stepped aside,
allowing Nick to enter the house. As he walked through the
threshold, a shiver ran down Nick's spine and his stomach
lurched, signaling the presence of a ghost, its energy prick-
ling the hairs on the back of his neck.

Shit.

"Nice place you've got here," Nick remarked, trying to
keep his voice calm. He glanced around the cozy living
room. "Your mom's decorating skills haven't diminished
since I was last here."

"Thanks, I'll be sure to tell her you approve." Ryan led
him towards the stairs. "My room's upstairs — that's where
all of the 'disturbances' have been happening." He made air
quotes around the word 'disturbances" with his fingers.

As they climbed the creaky wooden staircase, Nick felt
a sense of dread settling over him. Facing the unknown —
especially when it came to ghosts — still filled him with
anxiety. Then, his stomach lurched again and goosebumps
rose on his arms, a sure sign that a spirit was close by.

Ryan confidently swung open the door to his room.
"Here we are."

Posters of rock bands and sports teams plastered the walls, while clothes and textbooks lay scattered on the floor. Nick cautiously stepped inside, his gaze quickly landing on a mysterious figure lurking in the darkened corner. The dim lighting cast shadows over the unkempt room, adding an eerie atmosphere to their encounter.

"Nice room." Nick's voice faltered as he tried to maintain composure, his eyes fixated on the ghostly figure standing before him. The man appeared to be in his mid-thirties or early forties, with a gaunt face and hollowed cheeks. His translucent form seemed to flicker in and out of existence, giving off an eerie glow that illuminated the room. A chill crept up Nick's spine as the ghost stared back at him with empty, haunting eyes. Did this apparition mean harm, or was it simply lost in its spectral state? Whatever the reason, Nick couldn't deny the fear that gripped him in that moment.

"What are you staring at?" Ryan frowned, squinting at the empty space at which Nick was gazing.

"Right. Just my imagination playing tricks on me," Nick mumbled, turning his attention back to the apparition. It seemed to study Nick intently, as though sizing him up.

"Can you see me?" the specter asked. Its eyes grew wide. "You can! Oh my god, you can see me!"

"Who are you?" Nick mouthed, hoping Ryan wouldn't notice his sudden change in demeanor.

"I'm Scott," the ghost replied, his voice laden with regret. "I'm Ryan's father."

"His... father?" Nick gaped at the ghost. He'd never met Scott, but he'd heard from Ryan's stories that the man had been a heavy drinker and had caused a lot of pain to those around him.

"How is it you can see me and nobody else can?" Scott asked.

"Long story," Nick said. "It's an ability that runs in my family."

"What did you say?" Ryan asked.

Nick's voice trembled as he blurted out, "Ryan, I have to confess something. I'm aware this might sound crazy, but hear me out." He took a deep breath. "I can communicate with the dead. That's to say, I can see ghosts." Ryan's mouth dropped open in astonishment, as though unable to believe what he was hearing. Nick took a deep breath and continued, "There's a presence here with us right now. It claims to be Scott, your father. Apparently, he's been lingering around your room, watching over you since his passing." Ryan's face turned white as he struggled to process this shocking revelation.

"Are you for real?" Ryan scoffed, crossing his arms defensively. "My dad's dead, dude. He's never coming back."

"Trust me on this, alright?" Nick asked, a pleading note in his voice. "Just... hear what he has to say."

"Fine," Ryan grumbled, sitting down on the edge of his bed. He rolled his eyes in disbelief and sighed loudly. "I'll play your game. So, tell me Nick, what does my dead father want?"

Nick turned his head to Scott. "Now, I'm going to help you talk to Ryan — but you need to be honest with him about everything, okay?"

"I will. Then I'll be ready for my punishment. I realize I can't run away from it forever. I'm ready."

"Huh?" asked Nick. "What are you talking about?"

Scott's trembling voice echoed in the room, but only Nick had the capacity to hear it. "After I died, I saw this brilliant white light that was drawing me to it. But as I approached, a shadowy figure materialized in front of me, blocking my path. It was another ghost, one who had been stuck here for centuries, judging by the way he was dressed. He warned me that the light was a facade, a trick to lure unsuspecting souls into eternal torment on the other side. And he told me I would only face punishment because of the way I lived."

Nick's heart ached at Scott's words. He saw pain and terror in the ghost's eyes, but also regret and remorse.

"I don't want to suffer anymore," Scott continued, tears streaming down his cheeks. "But I accept that I deserve it. I was a horrible person. A terrible father. My addiction to alcohol consumed me and destroyed everything and everyone I loved."

"Listen to me," Nick said firmly, locking eyes with Scott. "That's not true. None of it. Your son never stopped loving you, and neither did anyone else who knew you. You have the power to find peace and redemption, but you have to let go of the guilt and self-loathing that's holding you back."

"But the years of drinking..." Scott said.

"You were struggling with addiction and made mistakes, but that doesn't define who you are as a person," Nick said. "And it certainly doesn't mean you deserve punishment."

A glimmer of hope flickered in Scott's eyes as he looked at Nick. "Really?" he asked.

"Really," Nick confirmed with a nod and a small smile. Together, maybe they could help Scott find the closure and forgiveness he desperately needed before moving on to whatever awaited him beyond this realm.

A sense of relief washed over Scott's face as he realized

there was still a chance for redemption. "Thank you, Nick," he whispered.

"Don't thank me yet," Nick replied with a small smile. "We have work to do."

"Oh my god, just fucking stop it, Nick!" Ryan said. "This is getting crazy. Dude, there's nobody there. You're talking to the air. I don't know what your end game is, but it's gone far enough. It's obvious you're making fun of me. This is a pretty sick fucking joke, if you ask me. I never would have pegged you for being such a dick."

Nick ignored Ryan and turned to Scott. "Can you share something that only you and Ryan are privy to? Something from his childhood, perhaps?" Nick's desperation was clear in his voice as he needed to prove that this wasn't some cruel joke on Nick's part.

Scott hesitated for a moment before speaking, his voice filled with remorse. "I used to take Ryan fishing down to Ripple Ridge Creek when he was a boy. He loved it, even though he never caught a thing. I'd bring him a can of his favorite soda — root beer — and a bag of chips every time. Sometimes even a candy bar. But one day, I got too drunk and forgot to bring them. Ryan said nothing. He just sat there with a sad look on his face. I felt like shit for days afterwards."

Nick repeated what the ghost had said.

Ryan's face paled.

The ghost continued. "Oh, and tell him that the first time he caught a fish, he was so horrified that he threw the entire pole into the creek. I never laughed so hard in all my life. But I never breathed a word of what happened to anyone."

"And he said that the first time you caught a fish, you

threw your fishing pole into the creek," Nick continued. "He laughed but never told a soul about it."

Ryan's eyes widened in disbelief as he turned to Nick. "How did you know all that? That's something only between me and my dad. We never even told my mom."

"It's because your dad just told me," Nick said. "Right here, right now."

Scott looked at his son, his face filled with regret. "I'm sorry, Ryan. I realize I messed up a lot when I was alive. But I've been watching over you since I passed on, and I want to tell you I'm proud of the man you've become. You're strong and resilient, and you've come so far since those days by the creek."

Nick told Ryan what his father had just said. Ryan's eyes were red and watery, his expression a mix of disbelief and joy as he stared at Nick. "So it's really true? My dad is here?"

Nick nodded. "He is."

Ryan looked up. "I miss you, Dad," he whispered, his voice thick with emotion.

Scott's spectral form flickered for a moment before solidifying, as though trying to reach out to his son. "I miss you too, Ryan," he whispered. "I just wish I could have done better when I was alive. I'm sorry for all the pain I caused."

"So, why are you frightening your son?" Nick asked the ghost.

"Ryan," Scott said, his face twisted in shame. "I couldn't bear to see him making the same mistakes I did — drinking, getting into trouble, hurting people. He's heading down the same destructive path I did. I was just trying to get his attention, to get him to stop."

"Your father loves you, Ryan," Nick relayed Scott's message. "He's haunted by the mistakes he made in life, and he doesn't want you to fall into the same patterns with alcohol and hurting people as he did. He says he'll always love you and that he's sorry for the pain he caused."

"I'll be okay," Ryan said. "When you died, it made me so sad and angry. I didn't mean to worry you." Ryan's eyes grew wide. "Ah, that explains the book."

"The book?" Nick asked.

"Yeah. I had a flask of vodka on the dresser next to my bed. I was sitting on my bed and when I opened it up to take a drink, a book that was sitting at my desk flew at my head." Ryan looked up. "Was that you Dad?"

Scott nodded.

Nick grinned. "Yeah, that was him."

Scott's spectral form flickered again, as though struggling to maintain its presence in the world of the living. "I wanted to make things right, but I was unsure of how to do it. I'm sorry for all the pain I caused you and your mother. Hopefully, you can find it in your heart to forgive me."

Nick told Ryan what his father said.

"Where is he?" Ryan asked Nick. Nick pointed to the corner of the room where Scott stood. Ryan cautiously approached the area to where Nick was pointing, tears streaming down his face. "I forgive you, Dad," he said, his voice choked with emotion. "I know you did the best you could. And I'm glad you're still here with me, even if it's in a different form."

Nick watched the emotional scene unfold, his heart aching from the pain and regret that saturated the room. Though he wasn't supposed to engage with any ghosts, Nick had done the right thing in coming here and telling Ryan about his father's presence. It wasn't often that ghosts had the chance to make amends with the living, and Nick was glad to have been a part of that reconciliation.

"Thank you," Scott whispered toward Nick, gratitude shining in his eyes. "How can I ever repay you for this?"

"Helping you find peace is repayment enough," Nick assured him.

Suddenly, the ghost gasped in awe. "The light...it's back! And it's so beautiful."

"No, wait!" Nick exclaimed, panic gripping his chest. "Don't go into the light! Leo might have set a trap!"

"Leo?" Scott frowned, pausing just before stepping into the light. "That name is familiar. I've heard others talk about him. Who is he?"

"A malevolent entity who's been kidnapping spirits," Nick said, shaking his head. "We're advising ghosts not to go into the light."

"Thank you," Scott whispered. "But I'll be okay. The shadow people who were blocking the light the last time are gone now. I think it's safe for me to cross over."

"Are you —" Nick said

"Tell my son I love him. And tell my wife I'm sorry."

"I will," Nick murmured, watching as the ghost disappeared into the light. A sense of relief washed over him — not only had he helped Scott find peace, but he'd also protected him from Leo's sinister machinations. "Goodbye, Scott. It was an honor to have met you."

The room suddenly was awash in a soft, supernatural glow, emanating from a portal of light that had opened briefly, a brilliant shaft that seemed to pierce the veil between worlds. Nick gasped and momentarily shielded his eyes. With all the ghosts he'd helped cross over, this was the first time he'd ever seen The Light. So, why was he seeing it now?

Ryan's father passed through this radiant gateway, his

features softening with peace as he stepped into the light, his form dissolving into the brightness until he was gone.

Nick breathed a sigh of relief when the ghost had crossed, with no sign of Leo.

"Goodbye?" Ryan exclaimed. "No, wait! Don't let him leave yet!"

Nick shook his head.

"Is he... gone?" Ryan asked hesitantly, his voice thick with emotion.

"Yeah, he's gone," Nick confirmed, placing a comforting hand on the boy's shoulder. "He crossed into the light. But he'll always be with you, Ryan, and someday you'll see each other again."

Ryan, overwhelmed by the finality of the farewell, sank onto his bed, his body shaking with sobs. He buried his face in his hands, tears streaming through his fingers.

Nick sat beside Ryan, placing a comforting hand on his shoulder. With a gentle voice, he spoke soothing words to Ryan, reminding him that his father had found peace, that his crossing into the light was a transition to a place free from pain and regret.

"You did well, Ryan," Nick murmured. "He needed you to be strong, and you were. Now he's at peace. Remember, he'll always be a part of you."

Ryan nodded but said nothing.

"It's okay to let go," Nick reassured him. "Letting go doesn't mean forgetting. It means accepting that his journey differs from yours now."

"Thanks, man," Ryan said, managing a weak smile. "I have no idea what I would have done without your help. But what did you tell my mom? She's not the type to believe in ghosts or any of that stuff."

Nick chuckled. "Nah, she thinks I'm some kind of peer youth counselor."

Nick stood in the dimly lit room, still feeling the warmth of Scott's gratitude as he crossed over. Ryan looked around, still seemingly dazed by the unspoken exchange between Nick and his father. Nick understood that, even though Ryan was unable to see or hear the ghost, the moment had touched him deeply.

"Hey, I'm going to get going," Nick said softly, patting Ryan on the back. "You should take some time to process all of this."

"Thanks, Nick," Ryan replied, his voice cracking. "I appreciate everything you did for me and my dad."

"Of course." Nick forced a smile, despite the weight he felt in his chest. He needed to think, to understand what had just happened and how it connected to the larger threat they were facing.

As he stepped out into the cool night air, the epiphany struck him with the force of a lightning bolt. He suddenly understood why Leo was so intent on trapping souls like Scott — and why he'd gone after Quinn.

It was because of their guilt and self-loathing. If Nick could erase that from a ghost, then the shadow demon wouldn't be able to stop them from crossing over. Leo and his minions were preying on the vulnerable, convincing the dead that they weren't worthy of moving on to the other side. And those who didn't cross over would join Leo's army, lured by promises of happiness and strength.

"Son of a bitch," Nick muttered under his breath. The realization sent a shudder down his spine, both for its implications and for the terrible truth it revealed about the nature of the enemy they were facing.

He fumbled for his phone and dialed Nate's number,

pacing back and forth on the front lawn. When a familiar voice answered, he didn't waste any time.

"Nate, it's Nick. I think I may have figured out the key to stopping Leo and his underlings," he blurted, his words tumbling over one another in his haste to share what he'd learned.

"Slow down, Nick," Nate replied, his calm tone a stark contrast to his own frantic energy. "Tell me what happened."

"Okay, so I just helped a friend of mine's dad cross over, right?"

"Nick! You shouldn't —"

"Yes, I know. But crossing over a ghost wasn't part of my plans. Believe me. It just kind of happened. But before he could cross over, I had to help him let go of his guilt and regrets," Nick explained, trying to steady his breathing. "And that's when it hit me — that's how the shadow demon is trapping these souls. Leo is convincing them they don't deserve to move on and that if they do enter the light, eternal torment and aguish will await them. So they join with Leo instead."

"Interesting," Nate mused, his voice tinged with a hint of concern. "So you're saying that if we can help these ghosts find peace, then maybe The Dark One won't be able to stop them from crossing?"

"Exactly," Nick confirmed, feeling a surge of hope as he spoke the words aloud. "And not only that, but it should also weaken Leo's army. If we can get to these souls, then we might actually stand a chance against this dark entity."

"Remarkable," Nick breathed, clearly impressed by Nick's revelation. "You may have stumbled upon the very thing that might turn the tide in our favor, Nick."

"Doesn't it make sense?" Nick pressed, wanting to be sure he wasn't just grasping at straws. "Think about it–fear, regret, and self-loathing are powerful emotions. It stands to reason that a dark entity like Leo would feed on them, using them to grow stronger and more dangerous."

"Indeed it does," Nate agreed. "We've always suspected that negative emotions played a role in Leo's power, but we've never been able to pinpoint exactly how he was doing it. But now, thanks to your epiphany, we may finally have the answers we've been searching for."

"Right," Nick said, his heart pounding with newfound determination. "So, what do we do now? How can we use this knowledge to stop Leo and save these souls?"

"First, we need to inform the rest of the psychic council," Nate replied, his voice firm. "Once everyone agrees, we can strategize about the best way to counteract Leo's influence and help these lost spirits find peace."

"Okay." Nick nodded, even though Nate couldn't see him. "I'll leave that to you, then. Just tell me if there's anything else I can do to help."

"Of course, Nick. And thank you — not just for this vital information, but also for the incredible compassion and courage you've shown throughout all of this," Nate said, sincerity ringing clear in his tone.

"Thanks, Nate. That means a lot." Nick swallowed hard, touched by his praise.

"But no more crossing over any spirits! I mean it, Nick. None. It's too dangerous."

Nick chuckled. "I won't. I promise."

"Alright then. Be safe."

With that, the call ended, leaving Nick standing alone, his thoughts swirling like a storm.

At least, he had given one ghost the peace and closure he so desperately needed. And that, he decided, was something worth holding onto.

CHAPTER FOURTEEN

Nick and Katrina strolled cautiously through the rain-soaked square, their senses keenly attuned to every sight, sound, and smell. The slick cobblestones sent shivers up Nick's spine with each step. Above them, the dilapidated buildings seemed to loom and leer, their warped wooden beams creaking ominously in the wind. But despite the oppressive atmosphere, a vibrant energy pulsed through the bustling market.

"Katrina," Nick began, his voice barely audible above the wind, "I have to tell you about the vision I had. I think you'll wanna hear this."

"Recently?" she asked, her brow furrowing with concern as she turned her attention fully to her companion. "What did you see? Were you finally able to dredge something up relevant to our dire situation?"

The name caught in his throat, a lump forming as he struggled to speak. "Leo," he managed to say, finally finding his voice. "He and his minions descended upon the square during the Founder's Day Celebration." He took a deep breath before continuing, the memories flooding back. "The chaos, the screams, the bloodshed... it was a scene straight out of a horror movie. The devastation was unimaginable, like something from an apocalyptic world."

As they continued their leisurely stroll, Nick's words painted a vivid picture of the square in his mind. He explained that in the vision, the square was transformed into a place of pure jubilation, festooned with vibrant banners and strings of twinkling lights that danced in the gentle breeze. At its heart stood a covered statue, eagerly awaiting its grand unveiling in honor of the town's founding. An infectious energy filled the air, as smiling faces mingled and laughter echoed off the surrounding buildings. However, Leo and his army of the undead soon interrupted this joyful scene, turning the once lively atmosphere into one of terror as they mercilessly cut down anyone in their path.

"Nick, I'm so sorry you had to see that," Katrina murmured as he finished recounting the gruesome details. "I can't imagine how awful it must have been."

He shook his head, trying to dispel the images that still haunted him. He gestured to the square. "The worst part is that I know this is where they'll attack," he said grimly. "There's no doubt in my mind. I've already shared this information with the psychics back at the lodge and they agreed with me. At least we're forewarned."

"To be forewarned is to be forearmed," she said, her voice firm. "We have to use this information to our advantage."

"Agreed," Nick said, "but what can we do? We can't exactly go to the mayor and tell him to cancel the celebration because a demon and his army will be attacking."

"Of course we can!" Katrina mused. "Though perhaps

we can come up with a more rational reason for our request."

"Alright, so any ideas on what to tell him?" Nick asked, running a hand through his tousled hair. "We can't exactly waltz into his office and say, 'Hey, there's a demon and his army coming to crash our party and we want you to cancel it.'"

"Obviously not in those words," Katrina replied, rolling her eyes playfully. A crease formed between her brows as she mulled over his words. "But we need to come up with a plausible explanation that will actually make him cancel the celebration."

"Perhaps we could say there's a risk of an avalanche?" Nick suggested, his brow furrowing in thought. "Or a sudden influx of wild animals? Wait...I know. How about bears? We could tell him there have been grizzly sightings in nearby towns."

Katrina couldn't help but laugh at his suggestions. "Nicholas, this is Gallowspine Mountains — those sorts of things happen all the time," she pointed out with a smirk. "We need something more... convincing, more compelling, more believable."

"Alright, how about this: we tell him that someone has made a terrorist threat against the event," Nick proposed. "And we wouldn't even be lying.

"Now that is a possibility," Katrina mused, her gaze following his. "We could try it. It's the best we've got. Let's do it now."

"Now?"

"If what you've told me is going to occur, we have little time to waste. Time is of the essence, as they say."

As they continued walking, Nick took in the details of the bustling square. Colorful stalls were being set up, filled with handmade crafts, local delicacies, and various games for the children. Laughter and excited chattering filled the atmosphere, only heightening Nick's sense of urgency.

In the center of the square stood the large, covered statue, the chief attraction for the upcoming celebration. Although still hidden beneath a heavy cloth, Nick could make out the rough shape of a man astride a horse, one arm outstretched triumphantly. He knew it represented Bartholomew Shard, the legendary founder of their village, but at the moment, all he could think about was the impending attack. He shivered at the memory of his vision.

Their footsteps echoed on the cobblestone path as they approached the Mayor's office, a charming brick building adorned with colorful flowers and intricate stained glass windows. The heavy wooden door creaked open, releasing the faint scent of old books and burning firewood.

"I hope he's in," Katrina said.

Mayor Samuelson's office, nestled on the second floor of Gallowspine Town Hall, exuded an air of practicality with its sturdy oak furniture and walls lined with historical photographs of the town. Morning light filtered through large windows, casting a soft glow over the room. The mayor, a burly man with a salt-and-pepper beard, leaned back in his leather chair, looking curiously at Nick and Katrina as they entered. The air smelled faintly of leather and the coffee that rested in a cup beside him.

"Nick! Katrina!" boomed Mayor Samuelson, his deep voice resonating through the room. "What brings you to my humble abode on this fine afternoon?"

"Hey, Mayor Samuelson," Nick began, doing his best to sound serious and concerned. "We've come to discuss an urgent matter regarding the Founder's Day Celebration."

"Urgent? Well, do have a seat," the Mayor said, gesturing to a pair of mismatched chairs in front of his desk. As they sat down, he leaned back in his own chair, steepling his fingers beneath his chin. "Now, what seems to be the problem?"

They took their seats. Katrina exchanged a quick, nervous glance with Nick before speaking. "Mayor, we've come across some information that concerns the safety of the Founder's Day Event. We think it might be best to consider postponing it."

Raising an eyebrow, the mayor clasped his hands on the desk. "Safety concerns? Is this about the weather forecast? You know how unreliable those forecasts are."

Nick leaned forward, his voice earnest. "It's not the weather, sir. We've received credible reports of a potential disturbance of a violent nature. It could escalate, possibly even leading to injuries among the attendees."

Mayor Samuelson looked skeptical. "A disturbance? This sounds highly speculative. Do you have any concrete evidence?"

Katrina tried a different angle. "It's the nature of the threat, Mayor. We believe it's best not to take any risks where public safety is concerned. The repercussions could be severe."

The mayor shook his head slowly, his expression firm. "I understand your concerns, but postponing Founder's Day on the basis of something this vague... It would cause chaos. The preparations have taken months. People have poured their hearts into this event."

Nick pushed, his tone slightly more insistent. "But the risk, Mayor —"

"I'm responsible for this town," the mayor cut in, his voice rising slightly. "I can't shut down our most important day based on rumors. Unless you bring me something concrete within the hour, the event goes on, as planned."

His decision was clear, leaving a palpable tension in the room. Nick and Katrina exchanged a look of frustration, their mission unaccomplished.

"Thank you for your time, Mayor. We hope for a peaceful day," Katrina said.

As Nick and Katrina stood to leave, Mayor Samuelson's voice halted them. "Wait — how exactly did you hear about this supposed threat?"

Katrina paused, caught off-guard. "Someone who has been reliable in the past approached us confidentially. It's someone connected to the event's security arrangements."

Nick added quickly, his tone supportive. "This person wouldn't raise the issue without serious cause."

The mayor leaned back, his eyes narrowing slightly as he assessed their responses. "Confidential, you say? That complicates things. I appreciate you coming to me, but again, without more concrete details, my hands are tied. As a public servant, you understand the position I'm in. Tell them to come see me in person to discuss it."

"Yes, sir, we understand," Katrina responded, maintaining a respectful tone. "We just felt it was our duty to pass on the concern."

"Thank you both for bringing these issues to my attention," he said firmly, "but the Founder's Day Celebration will proceed as planned. I assure you, everything will be fine." His demeanor reflected a mix of skepticism and concern. "But keep me informed. If this threat materializes into something more tangible, I'll take immediate action. And as a preemptive safety measure, I'll increase the security and police presence at the event and enforce a strict no-weapons policy for entry."

"Thank you, Mayor," Nick said, as they turned once more to leave, his mind racing with the need for a new strategy.

Mayor Samuelson nodded, his expression unreadable. "I always prioritize the safety of Gallowspine. Again, keep me updated on any new information."

Venturing out into the corridor, Nick and Katrina found themselves immersed in the muffled chatter of the town hall. The weight of the approaching event pressed heavily on Nick's shoulders. They needed a new plan, and they needed it fast.

"I didn't have high hopes that the mayor would listen to us," Katrina muttered as they exited the building, her jaw clenched. "But it was worth a shot. Now we need to regroup and come up with a new plan."

"How about if we try talking to the townspeople?" Nick suggested as they walked back through the bustling square. "If we can't convince the Mayor, maybe we can at least warn people and help prepare for what's coming. Try to keep them away from the festival."

Katrina nodded in agreement, her expression filled with resignation. "It's not much, but it's better than doing nothing." She let out a heavy sigh. "Though I have no idea what we'll tell them."

"We'll come up with something, Katrina. We have to."

CHAPTER FIFTEEN

THE GENTLE CLATTER OF SILVERWARE AND THE LOW hum of chatter filled every corner of La Cucina Di Angelo, a warm and inviting Italian restaurant nestled in the heart of downtown. A collection of vintage wine bottles adorned the walls, while vibrant paintings of rolling Tuscan landscapes brought a touch of rustic charm into the space. At the center of a long table sat Nick, surrounded by the seven psychics who had come together for a quiet dinner, the rest remaining at the lodge. The scent of freshly baked bread and simmering sauces filled the air, adding to the cozy ambiance of the restaurant.

As they sat around the table, Nick's glass tinkled against the others as he raised it up. The indistinct murmur of voices and clinking of silverware filled the air. "Here's to us," he said, his voice barely audible over the hum of conversations around them. The aroma of basil and garlic wafted from the plates in front of them, making his mouth water. "To the successes that lie ahead." Their glasses chimed together in a melodic harmony.

"Cheers!" they all echoed.

Maya's dark curls bounced as she laughed, her fork twirling strands of spaghetti coated in rich tomato sauce. "Finally, some good food to calm my premonition jitters," she joked.

"Let's focus on the positives," Nick said, offering an encouraging smile as he cut into his veal scallopini. "We're together, we're prepared —"

A sudden chill swept through the restaurant, snuffing out the warmth. The laughter and chatter evaporated instantly as if sucked away by an unseen force. Nick's hand stilled mid-cut, and the psychics exchanged uneasy glances. The air felt electric, charged with a foreboding energy.

"*Something's wrong*," whispered Jasper, his eyes darting around the room. His face paled as he saw the flicker of dark shadows in every corner.

"Everyone stay calm," Nick murmured, trying to maintain his composure. But beads of sweat formed on his forehead, betraying his fear.

It came without warning — a thunderous crash that shattered the peaceful ambiance. The front window exploded inwards, showering the diners with shards of glass. Screams pierced the night as the patrons scrambled for cover, their faces contorted in terror. Through the gaping jaws of the destroyed entrance, a figure stepped forward — ominous and cloaked in darkness.

Leo.

Dark shadows billowed behind him like a shroud of death, and his red eyes glinted with malice as he surveyed the chaos he had caused. The air hissed with energy as he approached the group, daring them to stand against him.

Leo spoke in a low growl, his voice laced with threats and promises of destruction. And with each word, the room grew colder and darker, until it seemed like all hope was lost.

But then, a blinding light erupted from within Alex, sending Leo flying back with a howl of pain. With renewed courage and strength, Nick joined in the battle against this malevolent force and built up a force field in his mind, just as the psychics had taught him. It was a fight for their lives now.

Leo's eyes burned brighter with rage, his cloak billowing around him like a tempest. He retaliated with a surge of dark energy, attempting to break through their defenses. But Nick and the psychics stood strong, their determination unwavering.

"Ah, gathered like lambs for slaughter." Leo's voice dripped with malice, his words bouncing off the walls of the restaurant like a menacing echo. "How lovely."

"Everybody down!" Nate shouted, pushing his chair back with such force it toppled over.

The psychics sprang into action, a symphony of chaos erupting around them. Tables flipped, chairs thrown, and glass shattered as they erected barriers with their minds. The air crackled with energy and the scent of burning wood as the telekinetic shields shimmered to life. But Leo's power was relentless, lashing out like whips and tearing through their defenses. His dark aura pulsated with malice as he unleashed wave after wave of deadly attacks. The psychics struggled to hold their defenses against his ferocious strength.

As the battle raged on, the restaurant became a battle-field of swirling elemental forces and crackling psychic energy. Tables toppled, sending plates and glasses crashing to the floor.

With a wicked grin, Leo summoned a gust of wind that

swept through the restaurant, knocking the psychics off balance and tearing down their defenses. The air thickened with debris and the scent of fear.

"Raphael, now!" Nate's command cut through the chaos, drawing all eyes to the thin young man standing across from Nick.

With a deep breath and laser-like focus, Raphael locked his gaze on Leo and channeled his power into a thick wall of psychic energy that materialized in front of them. The wall shimmered and sizzled as though it were on fire. Its intense heat radiated in waves, causing beads of sweat to form on their skin. With focused intensity, the wall advanced towards Leo, its sole purpose to stop him in his tracks.

But Leo was not easily defeated; with a flick of his wrist, he swatted away the wall as if it were nothing but a puff of air. It dispersed like mist, leaving the psychics vulnerable once again.

"Is this all you have?" Leo taunted, his form flickering as he moved with unnatural speed. His mocking laughter echoed through the chaos, sending chills down the spines of those who dared to challenge him. It seemed like nothing could stand in the way of his vicious attacks, leaving the psychics struggling to come up with a plan to stop him before it was too late.

Nick's heart rammed into his rib cage. He dodged a flying shard of glass, but not enough, feeling a thin line of blood trickle down his cheek.

"Eliza, shield!" cried out Sia, her voice laced with panic as she conjured a gust of wind to buffet Leo back.

Eliza furrowed her brow in intense concentration, her hands outstretched towards the group. A shimmering dome, almost invisible to the naked eye, enveloped them, pulsating with a bright, otherworldly energy. For a moment, it held strong against Leo's furious assault, glowing with resilience. But then, with a primal roar that shook the ground beneath their feet, he struck the dome with all his might. It shattered like fragile ice under the force of a sledgehammer, sending shards of light flying in all directions and leaving them vulnerable to Leo's wrath. Darkness closed in around them, suffocating and oppressive.

"Nick, your hands!" Nate's voice cut through the chaos, pointing Nick's attention to his hands. They glowed with a faint light, pulsing beneath his skin like a trapped fire trying to break free.

"Use it Nick!" Nate shouted above the roaring sounds of battle.

Leo advanced, tendrils of shadow writhing around him. A blast of energy surged from Leo, striking Sia, who had been weaving illusions to disorient the demon. She screamed, crashing into a wall and crumpling to the ground, motionless.

NO!" The anguished cry tore from Nick's throat . The light in his hands faded as quickly as it had appeared.

Leo paused in his attack, tilting his head as if listening intently to something only he could hear. "Interesting," he muttered, then, without another word or gesture, vanished into the night as abruptly as he'd arrived.

Silence fell, broken only by the ragged breaths of the psychics and the distant wail of approaching sirens.

"Is she —" began Maya, rushing to Sia's side.

"Alive, but unconscious," Raphael confirmed grimly, already pressing his jacket against her head wound.

"We need to get her to a hospital," Nick said, his mind reeling as he fumbled for his phone. "I'll call 9-1-1."

The once charming and cozy restaurant now lay in ruins. Overturned chairs and tables littered the floor, shattered glass covered the ground, and black scorch marks defaced the walls. The air was thick with the stench of smoke and burning wood. Mixed in was the pungent scent of spilled wine, its sweet aroma now overpowering as it mingled with the acrid stink of destruction.

"Leo wasn't trying to kill us," Nate said, his jaw clenched as he surveyed the damage.

The taste of ash and smoke coated the back of Nick's throat, making it hard to breathe. The lingering sweetness of the wine added a bitter aftertaste."What do you mean? He nearly killed all of us."

Nate shook his head. "No, this was only a test. He was testing our strength to gauge how much of a threat we are to him. The actual attack is still to come."

"Then we'll be ready for him," Nick replied, though doubt gnawed at his resolve.

"Remember when you faced that strange entity several months back?" Nate asked, his voice laced with concern as he locked eyes with Nick. "What was it he said to you about a connection?"

Nick's brow furrowed as he recalled the cryptic words of the shadowy figure. "You mean that creepy shadow guy? He said that the key is my heart's connection. Whatever that means."

Nate's gaze shifted to the ceiling as he pondered this information. "And that time you faced Leo and light shot out of your hands... Gabe was with you then, wasn't he?"

A chill ran down Nick's spine as he remembered the terrifying encounter. But then a realization dawned on him. "Gabe... you think he might be the key — my heart's connection?"

Nate's expression turned determined as he nodded. "I have a strong hunch that the two of you together is the key — the missing piece." He ran his fingers through his hair and sighed. "I hate to ask this of you and him, but I think we need him to come back to Gallowspine Mountains," he declared, determination steeling his features. "He might be our only salvation against these dark forces."

Hours later, after the adrenaline had faded and Sia's condition stabilized in the hospital, Nick made the call. He'd put it off, hesitating because he didn't want Gabe to come back, to put him in danger. But he knew Nate was right. Gabe just might somehow be the key to defeating Leo.

"Nick?" Gabe's surprised voice came through the phone.

Nick's voice was hoarse and strained as he spoke, the desperation in his tone evident. "Yeah, it's me," he said. "I hate to ask you of this but can you come back? We need you."

"You do?" Gabe replied, a hint of concern in his voice.

"As much as I want to keep you safe and have you stay far away from here, Nate thinks that you have something to do with all of this. Remember when I told you about that terrifying dude who could freeze me to the spot and speak into my mind?"

Gabe chuckled nervously. "How could I forget?"

"He told me that the key is my heart's connection. And now Nate seems to think that he was talking about you — that you're my heart's connection."

There was a moment of silence on the other end of the phone, tension mounting as they both waited for Gabe's response.

"Gabe?"

"I'm still here," came his steady reply. "Isn't this what I've always been telling you? That you need me Nick because it's the Nick and Gabe show, not just the Nick show."

Nick took a deep breath. "So, can you come back? Will you come back?"

"I'm there," Gabe answered without hesitation, his eagerness palpable even through the phone.

A note of caution crept into Nick's voice. "No, wait. Before you agree, I need to tell you something. Leo attacked us tonight at a restaurant and Sia, one of the psychics, got hurt pretty badly. Nate thinks he was just testing us, that the actual fight is yet to come." He paused, then added solemnly, "It was terrifying. I want you to be sure before agreeing. Dammit, I wish there was another way."

There was a long pause on the other end of the line. When Gabe's voice finally came, it was resolute. "I've never been more sure about anything in my life," Gabe whispered into the phone, determination and bravery shining through his words. "I ain't no runner Nick. I'll stand with y'all to face whatever this is. Whatever role I have to play in all of this, I'll do it."

A surge of relief flood through Nick, mingled with a deep sense of gratitude. "Thank you, Gabe," he whispered, his voice choked with emotion..

"No thanks necessary. We're in this together."

"And Gabe... Don't tell your parents you're coming back. They wouldn't understand. You can stay at the lodge with the others until this is over."

"Roger that," Gabe said gravely. "See y'all soon."

Nick ended the call, staring out the hospital window at the night sky. With Gabe's impending return, a flicker of hope stirred within him. Nick knew deep down in his gut that having Gabe return to Gallowspine Mountains was the right decision.

CHAPTER SIXTEEN

THE RUSTIC CHARM OF THE WHISPERING WILLOW, THE town's most beloved eatery, was never more appreciated by Nick than now. Nestled in the heart of Gallowspine Mountains, its wooden beams and low-hanging iron chandeliers exuded a warmth that seemed to ward off the chill of dread that clung to him like a second skin. The restaurant buzzed with the soft chatter and clinking of cutlery.

Nick slid into a secluded booth at the back, his eyes scanning across the dimly lit interior, taking in the flickering candles on each table that cast dancing shadows upon the walls. He needed this moment, this semblance of normalcy, after everything that had transpired. Yet even here, amidst the scent of freshly baked bread, tension coiled within him, wound tight as a spring.

Nick tried to focus on his dining companions, but his senses were tuned elsewhere. With every creak of the entrance, his shoulders tensed. Maya was saying something about an art exhibit she had visited once, but Nick riveted his attention on the door. His thoughts drifted to the incident at the other restaurant — the night Leo had burst through the doors like a tornado, leaving chaos in his wake. Now, each laugh too loud or shadow too swift made Nick's heart hammer against his chest. He was safe here, or at least he tried to convince himself of that, as he sat there scanning every face that entered.

"Earth to Nick," a voice drew him back from his reverie. Eliza, her auburn hair pulled back in a practical ponytail, waved a hand before his eyes. "You're a million miles away."

"Sorry," he mumbled, offering a weak smile. "Just... a lot on my mind."

"Understandable," Jasper chimed in, sliding into the seat opposite Nick. His deep-set eyes were pensive, a stark contrast to his usually mischievous glint. "But we need to focus. We've got a small window to prepare for Leo's next move."

"Right," Nick nodded, his resolve hardening. "So, based on my vision, Nate is certain that Leo will strike during the Founder's Day celebration."

"Everyone seems to think so," Maya agreed, her voice carrying the slight accent that always reminded Nick of distant lands. "This would be right up his alley — maximum chaos and fear to feed off of."

"Which means we have to figure out his potential entry points, escape routes, everything." Nick's hands fidgeted with the napkin, twisting it in knots.

"Hey," Eliza reached over, placing her hand atop his. "We'll manage. Have faith."

"First things first," Jasper began, leaning forward, elbows on the table. "We need to map out the town square, identify strategic positions. We can't predict exactly how he'll come at us, but we can prepare ourselves on all fronts."

"Agreed," Maya nodded, her eyes scanning the room as if already envisioning the layout of the town square.

A server approached, breaking the intensity of their planning with an offer to take their orders and they provided their selections with polite smiles.

"Let's eat and then head out," Eliza suggested. "Clear heads work better when the belly isn't running on empty."

"True that," Nick conceded, allowing himself to relax ever so slightly as plates of food arrived. For a moment, they indulged in the flavors, the conversation drifting to lighter subjects, laughter mingling with the hum of the restaurant.

"Alright," Jasper said once they'd finished, determination lacing his words. "We've got until sundown to get a lay of the land. Let's split up — cover more ground."

"Sounds good," Eliza replied, wiping her mouth with a napkin. "I'll take the north side. I'm guessing he might use the old clock tower. It has a clear view of the entire square."

"Jasper and I will take the east and west sides," Maya stated. "We'll meet back here in two hours?"

"Two hours," Nick confirmed, his gaze sharpening as he looked at each of them. "Be careful. Leo may be already watching the square."

"Always am," Jasper said with a wry grin that didn't quite reach his eyes.

"Stay alert," Maya added, her tone carrying the weight of experience.

"Will do," Eliza promised, standing up from the booth with a stretch.

They each went their separate ways, leaving the cozy confines of the restaurant behind. The cool evening air brushed against Nick's skin as he stepped outside, the sky painting itself in hues of orange and pink as the sun began its descent.

He walked through the town square, noting the preparations for the Founder's Day celebration — the streamers, the stage setup, the anticipation in the air. His mind raced with what-ifs, the scenarios playing out with each step he took.

His boots clicked against the cobblestone as he moved stealthily, mapping out each alleyway, each possible vantage point in his pocket notebook. He could almost hear Leo's taunting laugh, feel the malevolence that would soon descend upon this place. But Nick wouldn't let fear take hold — not when there was still a chance to stop whatever twisted game Leo was playing.

"Surveillance cameras," he muttered, making a mental note of their locations. "Have to check if they're working."

His mind worked through the logistics, the strategies, the constant drive to stay one step ahead of an enemy who thrived on unpredictability. Every shadow seemed suspect, every whisper of wind a potential warning. He jotted down more notes in his notebook, determined not to miss a single detail.

"Gotta keep everyone safe," Nick thought, his fingers pausing over the screen. "Can't let the demon win."

As the sky darkened and the appointed hour neared, Nick made his way back to The Whispering Willow. The others were already there.

"Find anything of interest?" he asked, sliding back into the booth.

"Potentials," Jasper replied, unfolding a map of the square. "We'll have to cover these areas."

"Cameras are all functioning, but we should monitor them," Eliza added, tapping a finger on the map where she had noted the locations. "Make sure nobody tampers with them."

"Good," Nick nodded, his thoughts turning inward once again.

"Leo won't know what hit him," Maya said, a fierce light burning in her eyes.

Nick agreed but based on what happened the other night at the restaurant, he couldn't help but wonder how in the hell they were going to pull this off.

NICK'S REFLECTION in the windowpane of his room seemed to waver with the rippling shadows cast by the fire flickering in the hearth. He sat on the edge of his bed, the phone cradled between his shoulder and ear as he waited for the familiar voices to pierce through the silence.

"Nick? Nick, is that you?" His mother's voice, tinged with both relief and worry, finally broke through.

"Hey, Mom. Yeah, it's me," he said, his voice steady despite the turmoil he felt inside.

"Hold on. Let me put you on speakerphone." A couple of clicks came through the phone's speaker. "Can you hear me?"

"Yup," he said. "You're a bit echoey, but you're coming through loud and clear."

"Your father, sister and I are at —"

"Nuh, uh, uh," Nick said.

"Oh, that's right," she said. "I forgot that I'm not supposed to tell you. So, how are things over there?" Her words were casual, but an undercurrent of concern threaded through them.

"Everything's quiet for now. We're just... getting ready," Nick replied, intentionally vague. He couldn't — wouldn't — tell them about Leo's ambush at The Whispering

Willow. They were safe and far away; they didn't need that fear.

"Good, good. We've been so worried since we left, wondering if you're alright," his dad chimed in, his deep voice resonating with barely concealed anxiety.

"Really, I'm fine, Dad." Nick traced the grain of the wood on the nightstand with his finger, feeling the rough texture. "We have a plan."

"Missy's here with us," his mom added, changing the subject. "She... she saw another ghost yesterday, but she's handling it better. For now, she pretends not to see them."

Nick let out a soft sigh, imagining his little sister putting on a brave face. "She's tough. Just tell her I said to keep up the good work and stay strong. Tell her I'll teach her everything I can when you all get back."

"Will do. And Nick, please, please, please be careful," his mother said, her voice breaking slightly.

"I will. Promise."

After they exchanged a few more words of reassurance and love, the call ended with a click that sounded too final for Nick's liking. He dropped the phone onto the bed and ran a hand through his hair — a gesture of frustration and resolve.

He stood and walked over to the window, pressing his palm against the cool glass, gazing out into the night. A part of him wished he could confide everything to his parents, unburden his heart of the dread and determination mingling within. But he knew better. They had enough to worry about.

"Can't let Leo win," he murmured to himself, his breath fogging up a small circle on the window where his forehead rested. "Can't let Leo win."

A knock at the door jolted him from his thoughts. He

straightened up, swiping at his eyes, and called out, "It's open."

The door swung inwards, revealing Gabe standing there, a duffel bag slung over his shoulder and an uncertain smile playing on his lips. His presence filled the room with an energy that seemed to brighten even the dimmest corners.

"Hey," Gabe greeted, stepping inside. He set down his bag and Nick rushed across the room and into Gabe's open arms. They shared a long kiss that mingled the taste of longing with relief. They pulled apart, and both smiled.

"Hey yourself," Nick beamed, all traces of his earlier worries momentarily forgotten. "I wasn't expecting you until tomorrow," he whispered. "I am so glad to see you."

"Me too. Figured I could help out sooner rather than later. Hope it's okay that I'm early?"

"More than okay," Nick assured him, nuzzling his face in Gabe's neck.

When they pulled apart, Nick grasped Gabe's hand briefly, letting the moment linger.

"Crash here tonight?" Nick asked, nodding towards the bed.

Gabe flashed him a sly grin. "I figured I'd ask first, but yeah, if that's cool with you."

"Of course, it's cool. More than cool."

The conversation shifted to lighter topics as they settled into the room. They talked about the town, the upcoming Founder's Day celebration, Gabe's grand-mother, and the mundanities of life that seemed so precious now.

Nick turned to Gabe, a mix of emotions swirling within — gratitude for the love of the boy beside him, and a rekin-dled sense of purpose for the coming fight.

"Come here," Gabe murmured, pulling Nick into another embrace.

"Thank you," Nick whispered, burying his face in Gabe's shoulder. "For being here. For everything."

"Always," Gabe whispered back, tightening his hold.

THE LOW HUM of conversation filled the downstairs dining room. Nick and Gabe sat in the sitting room, adjacent to the dining room. Warm light pooled from the side table lamps, casting a soft glow in the room.

"Nick," Gabe began tentatively, his voice barely more than a murmur above the ambient noise. "What if my parents see me at the Founder's Day event? They always attend. They think I'm still at my grandma's house — unless she told them I left. I told her not to tell them but you never know."

Nick glanced at Gabe, noting the furrow between his brows, the way his fingers tapped an anxious rhythm on the tabletop. He paused and swallowed.

"Then we'll deal with it," Nick replied, reaching out to still Gabe's hand with his own, noticing the tremor beneath his touch.

"Maybe I should just tell them I'm back," Gabe suggested. "It's not like I can avoid them forever."

"Perhaps," Nick agreed hesitantly, considering the ramifications. "But if you do, they'll ask questions. About why you're back. Maybe about us." He let the words hang in the air, heavy with meaning.

Gabe drew in a deep breath and exhaled slowly, his gaze settling back on Nick. "I get that. But what about the psychics? We can't risk exposing them, either."

"Let's talk to them," Nick decided. "See if they have any ideas on how to keep you under the radar for now."

Pushing through the door to the private room reserved for their meetings, Nick and Gabe walked in and greeted Maya, who always appeared to be working there.

"Nick, Gabe," acknowledged Maya, her eyes sharp and calculating. "What's up?"

"Gabe's parents," Nick said, nodding towards Gabe. "They might see him at the Founder's Day celebration."

"Ah." Maya pursed her lips, and the others exchanged glances. "We'll need to be discreet, then. Perhaps a minor glamour, something to alter perceptions without drawing attention."

"Can you do that?" Gabe asked, hope threading through his voice.

"Consider it done," confirmed Paolo, who sat across from Maya. "We'll do it before the event. But it will only be a temporary measure and there's no knowing how long it will last. But eventually, you'll need to decide how to handle your parents."

"Thank you," Gabe said, a grateful smile pulling at his lips.

"Let's focus on the more pressing matter at hand," Maya interjected, steering the conversation back to strategy. "Leo's attack."

Nick nodded, his thoughts momentarily shifting from personal concerns to their collective mission. They spent the next hour poring over maps of the town square, pinpointing potential hotspots, discussing escape routes and contingencies. All the while, Nick couldn't shake the image of Gabe's parents, their reactions, their possible hurt and anger at being kept in the dark.

After the meeting, Nick retreated to the small patio

outside the main dining room, needing air, needing space to reflect. He needed advice. So he dialed his mom's number, watching the way the moon dangled low in the sky, its silver light bathing the world in a gentle luminescence.

"Nick? Is everything alright?" His mom's voice crackled through the phone, laced with concern.

"Yeah, Mom, everything's fine," he assured her, though his chest tightened with the lie. "Just needed to hear your voice."

"And how's Gabe? Is he okay?"

"Actually, Mom, that's part of why I called," Nick admitted, rubbing the back of his neck. "We're... worried about his parents finding out he's back."

"Oh, they're unaware he's back?" she asked, confusion clear in her tone.

"It's complicated," Nick sighed. "There's a lot they don't know about what he's been up to. Like the ghost stuff, for instance."

"Oh, honey," his mom breathed out, a note of empathy in her voice. "If I were in their shoes, I'd want to know. Regardless of whether I liked what I heard. It's dangerous, Nick, what you're all involved in. They have a right to know about their son, especially given the circumstances."

"So, you're saying he should tell them?" Nick asked, the idea daunting yet somehow freeing.

"Whether or not they accept it, at least they'll understand why he's here," she said softly. "And they deserve that much truth."

"Thanks, Mom," Nick said, a strange sense of resolve taking shape. "I love you."

"Love you too, sweetheart. Stay safe."

He ended the call, pocketing his phone, and looked up at the stars scattered across the velvet night sky. Turning back inside, he found Gabe waiting for him, the question in his eyes clear.

"My mom says you should tell them," Nick said, closing the distance between them. "About everything. She said that she'd want to be informed if she was your mom."

Gabe's Adam's apple bobbed as he swallowed, nodding slowly. "You're right," he said, determination steeling his features. "Okay, I'll do it. I'll tell them."

Nick wrapped an arm around Gabe's shoulders, drawing him close. In the end, it was about facing the truth, however difficult or frightening.

"I can't believe the Founder's Day celebration is only forty-eight hours away," Nick said. "Earlier when we were there, the vendors were already hauling in their wares and setting up booths. There's everything from homemade pies to handcrafted jewelry."

"I wonder if they'll have the apple bobbing again this year," Gabe said. His voice carried a hint of forced levity, but the tension in his shoulders betrayed him.

"Probably," Nick replied, turning to flash a quick smile at Gabe. "You were the reigning champ three years running before you left."

"Seems like a lifetime ago." Gabe's gaze lingered on the town square below. "I bet my mom will organize the raffle again, like she always does."

"Have you decided when you're going to talk to them?" Nick asked, shifting his weight from one foot to the other. He wanted to take some of the burden off Gabe's shoulders, but he understood this was a path Gabe had to walk alone.

"Tonight," Gabe said, exhaling sharply. "I can't go into Founder's Day with that hanging over me. But I'm not looking forward to it. How do you tell your mom that you're going to battle a demon and his army of the dead? Heck, she may try to have me locked up."

"Hey," Nick said gently, reaching out to squeeze Gabe's arm, "whatever happens, I'm here for you. You realize that, right? And you can always tell them to call my mom if they want to talk about it with someone."

Gabe nodded, the corners of his mouth quirking up in a semblance of a smile. "I know, Nick. That means everything to me."

Nick pulled out his phone and flicked at the screen. He handed his phone to Gabe. "Here's my mom's cell. Add it to your contacts so that your folks can call her if they want to talk it over with an "adult.""

Gabe typed the number into his phone. "Thanks man. That might help."

"What do you say we head down to the restaurant, grab a piece of pie?" Nick suggested, hoping to distract Gabe for a little while. "We can plan our strategy for the square over something sweet."

"Sounds good," Gabe agreed.

They made their way down to the bustling street, side-stepping ladders and dodging decorators with bundles of streamers. The cafe was a cozy establishment, its brick walls covered in ivy that turned fiery red with the season. Inside, the ambiance was a warm juxtaposition to the crisp autumnal air outdoors.

"Table for two, please," Nick requested, and the host led them to a quiet corner booth draped in soft golden light from an overhead lantern.

"Thanks for being here," Gabe said, his voice low as they sat across from each other. "I couldn't face all this without you."

"Where else would I be?" Nick smiled, trying to infuse

some confidence into the moment. Their server's arrival interrupted them, a young woman with a friendly smile who took their order and promised to return shortly with their drinks.

"Okay, so the psychics are going to do another sweep of the square tomorrow," Nick began once they were alone again, unfolding his napkin onto his lap. "They'll set up some protective wards and energy barriers, but we'll need to stay alert."

"Right," Gabe concurred. "And we have to assume Leo knows we're aware of his Founder's Day plans. I hope he doesn't, but it's best to assume he does."

"Which is why we can't let our guard down, not even for a second," Nick added, his fork tracing patterns on the white tablecloth. "It's not just about us anymore. This is our town; these are our people."

"Speaking of 'our people'..." Gabe trailed off, biting his lip. "Telling my parents about the ghost stuff — it's going to change everything. They might not even believe me."

"Your truth is your truth, Gabe," Nick said firmly. "How they react doesn't change what's real. And who knows, they might surprise you."

Gabe chuckled humorlessly. "I guess I'll find out soon enough."

Their pie arrived, accompanied by two scoops of vanilla ice cream. They ate mostly in silence, the clink of cutlery punctuating their thoughts more than words ever could. Nick watched Gabe push his pie around his plate, his appetite apparently overcome by nerves.

"Remember that time we snuck onto the Ferris wheel?" Nick asked suddenly, a memory surfacing from the depths of happier days.

Gabe looked up, a flicker of amusement in his eyes.

"And we were certain we'd be stuck up there forever because the operator caught us and stopped it, just to punish us? I was so freaked out!"

"Yet here we are," Nick said, "facing something much scarier than an angry carnie." He reached across the table, covering Gabe's hand with his own. "We've got this, Gabe. Together, always."

"Always," Gabe echoed, squeezing Nick's hand.

CHAPTER SEVENTEEN

Nick sat in the common room of the lodge, sprawled on the faded plaid sofa, his legs stretched out before him, one foot tapping an anxious rhythm into the worn wooden floor.

Gabe entered the common room like a specter, his usually bright blue eyes clouded over, movements as heavy as if he were wading through molasses. He sank into the armchair opposite Nick with a sigh that seemed to carry the weight of mountains.

"Hey," Nick said softly, his foot ceasing its rhythmic dance. "How'd it go?"

Gabe's laugh was hollow, devoid of any genuine humor. His eyes were puffy. "Oh, you know," he started, voice laced with bitter irony, "a violent volcanic eruption at its finest."

"Uh-oh. That bad, huh?" Nick ventured, already knowing the answer.

"Understatement of the year." Gabe ran a hand through his disheveled hair, a gesture of frustration Nick had come to recognize all too well.

"Come on, tell me everything," Nick urged, leaning forward, elbows on his knees.

Gabe recounted the events with a detached air, as if he were reporting someone else's tragedy. His parents had asked him why he was back in town after he had just left, and for a moment, hope had flickered in his chest like a candle in the wind.

Gabe's words trembled on the edge of his lips, carrying a weight he had been carrying for far too long. His hands clenched and unclenched nervously as he recounted the moment to Nick.

"I told them I had something important to say," Gabe began, his voice catching on the first words. The air was tense and heavy with anticipation, like a brewing storm ready to unleash its fury.

"I just... said it. 'I'm gay.'" Gabe's voice cracked, and he paused to clear his throat. "It's strange how it all happened. I hadn't planned on telling them about us, about being gay, I mean. My only plan was to explain the ghost thing. But it just came out."

Gabe met Nick's gentle press for more information with a wry smile, but it didn't reach his eyes. "Explosions would have been quieter," he said with a bitter laugh. "They screamed at me, told me I was disgusting, filthy, and that I was a disgrace to the family. Said I was going to burn in hell for eternity and that I was no longer their son. And then they told me I should never come back to their house, that I was no longer welcome there. Ever."

"Jesus, Gabe..." Nick's heart clenched at the pain in his friend's voice. "I'm so sorry."

"Me too," Gabe whispered, staring into the fire as if it could burn away the hurt. "You know the worst part? I didn't even get to warn them about the ghosts and the danger that's lurking here."

"Hey, it's okay. We'll figure it out together," Nick assured him, reaching a hand out, hovering between them, unsure.

"Thanks." Gabe offered a weak grin, accepting the unspoken support in Nick's gesture. "I should have known that this would have been their reaction given how crazy religious they are. I never thought they'd throw me out and say such terrible things to me, though." He wiped at a tear that rolled down his rosy cheeks. "So, what now?"

"Let me call my parents and ask them if you can stay with us when this is all over. I'm sure they'll be fine with it. They adore you, Gabe."

Gabe's eyes flickered with a mix of relief and uncertainty as he nodded. "Thank you, Nick. I don't know what I would do without you."

Nick squeezed Gabe's hand reassuringly. "You don't have to worry about that. We're in this together, remember?"

Gabe managed a small smile, his shoulders slowly easing the weight they had carried since his confrontation with his parents. "Yeah, I remember."

As they sat in the dimly lit common room, a surge of anger towards Gabe's parents flooded through Nick. How could they turn their backs on their own son so heartlessly? It made him grateful for his own parents.

But dwelling on anger wouldn't change the situation. Gabe needed support now more than ever.

"I'll make the call right now," Nick said, his voice filled with determination. He reached for his phone on the side table, ready to dial his parents' number. As he pressed the buttons, he couldn't shake off the heaviness of the situation.

It wasn't fair that Gabe's family rejected him simply because of who he loved.

The phone rang, and Nick's parents answered with their usual warmth and concern. "Hey, Mom, Dad," Nick greeted them, his voice trembling.

"Three times in one day," his mother said. "Do you miss us or something?"

"I do, but I need to talk to you about something super important."

"What is it, sweetie?" His mom asked, her tone shifting to a serious one. "Is everything okay there?" Nick could hear his dad in the background, letting Nick know they were on speakerphone.

Nick paused for a moment before blurting out the words. "It's about Gabe. His parents kicked him out of their house after he came out as gay. He has nowhere to go."

There was a deep intake of breath on the other end of the line. "Oh my goodness," his mom gasped, her maternal instincts kicking in. "That poor boy. Is he okay?"

"Not really," Nick replied, tears welling up in his eyes. "He's scared and upset." He cleared his throat. "So I was wondering —"

"Of course we'll help him," his dad said decisively. "Tell him he'll stay with us. He's always welcome in our home, no matter what. We'll make sure he has a safe place to stay."

Tears now streaming down his face, Nick couldn't believe how lucky he was to have such loving and accepting parents. "Thank you, thank you so much," he choked out.

His mom chimed in, her voice gentle and compassionate. "Of course, sweetheart. We love Gabe like he's our own son. Tell him not to worry. We'll take care of him."

Relief washed over Nick, tears welling in his eyes. "Thank you," Nick whispered, struggling to keep his voice steady. "You don't know how much this means to both of us."

His parents assured him they understood, their voices filled with unwavering support, and said that they would make all the arrangements for Gabe to stay with them when they got back — but he and Nick need to be in separate bedrooms until they turned eighteen. They exchanged a few more words of comfort before Nick ended the call, a weight lifted off his shoulders.

"Gabe," Nick turned to his boyfriend, whose eyes were still fixed on the fire. "My parents said you can stay with us. They want you there."

Gabe's eyes flickered with a mix of gratitude and vulnerability. "Are you sure?"

Nick squeezed Gabe's hand gently. "Believe me, if they didn't, they would have told me. They consider you family, Gabe, and family sticks together, no matter what."

A hint of a smile tugged at the corner of Gabe's lips as he finally looked up at Nick. "Thank you."

"But..." Nick hesitated. "We can't share a bed."

"I figured as much." Gabe's face fell slightly, but he quickly masked it with a chuckle. "But we'll always have the cabin, right?"

"Yup...and you know," Nick said, wiggling his eyebrows, "my parents aren't home *all* the time. So they'll be plenty of chances for us to be — ahem — alone."

Gabe laughed. "I like the way you think, Mr. Michelson." He took in a deep breath. "And thank you, Nick. For everything."

"Always, man." Nick meant every word, and in that moment, their bond felt solid and enduring.

"Let's not waste this evening," Gabe suggested with a

glimmer of his former self. "How about a game of Texas Hold'em?"

"Sounds good," Nick agreed, relieved to have something to focus on. "But just so you know, I've been honing my poker skills."

"Bring it on," Gabe said with a smirk, finally standing up. He moved to the shelf where the games were kept, his back to Nick for a moment.

Nick watched as Gabe busied himself with the cards. He admired Gabe's courage, the strength it took to stand in one's truth even when faced with such heartrending consequences. A fierce protectiveness surged within him, a determination to shield his friend from any further harm.

"Ready to lose miserably?" Gabe taunted, returning with the deck of cards in hand.

"In your dreams," Nick shot back, the playful banter easing the tension that clung to the edges of the evening.

As they settled into the game, laughter and the soft sound of shuffling cards filled the room. For the time being, the world outside — with its haunting secrets and harsh realities—would have to wait.

NICK SAT HUNCHED over on an old, moth-eaten sofa in the common room, his eyes tracing the intricate patterns of the faded Persian rug beneath his feet.

Across from him, the psychics — Madame Celeste and her apprentice, Jasper, huddled over a cluttered table, strewn with thick books and yellowed papers.

"Here," Madame Celeste's voice cut through the quiet, "We've found something."

Nick's head snapped up, his body tensing as if

preparing for a fight. "About Leo?" he asked, his voice hoarse with anticipation.

"Indeed," she said, smoothing out a creased page with a bony finger. "Leo... Leopold Barnett," she murmured to herself, her voice a mere whisper in the silence.

A photo slipped from between the pages, landing softly on her lap. She picked it up, examining the black-and-white image of a young man with an unassuming face — clean-shaven, hair neatly parted to one side. His eyes held a glimmer of something untamed, a foreshadowing of the darkness that would soon consume him. She held up the photo to Nick.

"Oh my god, that's him!" Nick exclaimed. "That's the guy — the demon — I encountered and who attacked us at the restaurant. He's even wearing that same damn red base-ball cap."

"It appears our Leo was quite ordinary at the start, a boy of the 1940s," she said. "But then...he left home at sixteen. And from this point forward, his life took a turn into darkness."

"Black Magic," Jasper interjected, pushing his round glasses up the bridge of his nose. "He embraced practices most would fear to even whisper about."

"Spells woven with such finesse they were deemed impossible by even seasoned practitioners," Madame Celeste said.

Nick leaned forward, resting his elbows on his knees. His thoughts churned like the storm clouds gathering outside the window. Leo, a regular person turned corrupt? It was almost too much to wrap his head around.

"What else does it say?" Nick demanded, the urgency in his voice betraying his calm exterior.

"Leo discovered an aptitude for the arcane arts,"

Madame Celeste continued, her eyes not leaving the text before her. "An innate talent for casting spells that many seasoned practitioners could not fathom."

"Spells that corrupted him," Jasper added, a shudder visibly going through his slight frame. "The sources indicate that the black magic rotted his soul, made him into something...other."

"Exactly," she said. "Leo's descent into black magic wasn't gradual; it was a plummet. Power seduced him, and with each forbidden spell cast, his soul darkened like fruit left to wither on the vine."

"Rotted his soul?" Nick repeated, an icy dread settling in his stomach. "How does someone come back from that?"

"Perhaps they don't," Madame Celeste mused. "Perhaps they simply become something else entirely."

"Something powerful," Jasper whispered. "And deadly."

"Powerful enough to cast a spell to extend his influence beyond death," Madame Celeste said, locking eyes with Nick. "And since he passed, he's been accruing strength, amassing souls..."

"Decades of power," Nick murmured, his mind racing. The pieces of the puzzle were coming together, forming an image more terrifying than any ghost story. Leo hadn't simply passed on; he'd forged himself into something else entirely before he even died. A being that transcended mortality, hungering for power and souls across decades. He had been planning this, building his strength for years, and now they were caught in his web.

"Exactly," Madame Celeste confirmed. "Which means we are not dealing with a mere malevolent spirit. We are confronting an entity that has had time to grow, to learn, to ensnare. Leo had not merely sought power in life; he's ensnared it beyond death's veil. His machinations did not finish with his last breath — they were only just beginning."

A sudden gust of wind rattled the windowpanes, causing Madame Celeste to startle and glance around. The room felt charged now, as if her discoveries had somehow bridged a gap between past and present. She closed the book with reverence tinged with unease. "It was sheer luck I stumbled across this book in a dusty old bookshop in the next town. Or perhaps the universe guided me to it." She stood up, tucking the photograph into her pocket as if keeping it close could anchor her to reality against whatever phantasmal tide might be rising. "Whatever it was, it fell into our hands. Thankfully. Jasper and I studied it all afternoon."

"Then what's the next move?" Nick asked, clenching his fists. "How do we fight something like that?"

"Knowledge is our first weapon," Madame Celeste replied. "Understanding Leo's past is paramount. We must unravel the nature of the spell he cast upon himself and find its weakness."

"Every spell has its counter," Jasper chimed in, his youthful face set with determination. "No magic is infallible. Or so they say."

"So, we keep digging, right?" Nick asked, standing up and pacing the room. "We can't let him keep doing this — gathering souls. We have to stop him."

"Indeed, but caution, young man," Madame Celeste warned. "We must tread carefully. Leo will sense our intentions. He's bound to the very fabric of this place, after all."

"Let him sense it," Nick spat out, the fire reflecting in his eyes. "I'm not afraid of him."

"Bravery and recklessness walk a fine line, Nick," Jasper said softly. "We must be strategic."

"Jasper is right," Madame Celeste agreed. "We proceed with both courage and prudence. Our lives, and the souls of many, hang in the balance."

Nick stopped pacing and looked at them. Of course, they were right. This wasn't just some vengeful spirit — it was a battle against a force that had been gaining momentum for over half a century.

"Alright," Nick conceded, the weight of his own fervor settling into a more tempered resolve. "So what do we do next?"

"From what I've gathered," Jasper began, shifting through the scattered papers in front of him, "we need to identify the exact nature of Leo's spell. If we can understand the components, perhaps we can dismantle it."

"Or at least disrupt it," added Madame Celeste, her eyes narrowing with thought. "There may be a ritual or a counter-charm that could weaken his hold on this place and the souls he's captured."

"Which means we need to find out more about his life," Nick pointed out, "specifically when he started practicing black magic. There has to be some record, something written, maybe even a personal diary. I remember Katrina saying that some magicians keep a magical diary or grimoire. Maybe we could hunt down Leo's?"

"Indeed," Jasper agreed. He pulled out a thick, leather-bound tome from his bag, setting it gently on the coffee table. "Oh, and I found this today at the town library. It's a compilation of local history, including notable figures from the past century." He flipped through the pages, stopping at a section marked with a yellowed piece of paper. "Here, listen to this."

Madame Celeste and Nick leaned in as Jasper read aloud an excerpt about a young man named Leo who'd left his family home at the age of sixteen under mysterious circumstances. The text was vague, but further on, there were reports of a figure matching his description involved in unsettling incidents around town — incidents that locals whispered were tied to the forbidden arts.

"Black magic..." Nick muttered, piecing together the timeline. "He must have been drawn to it, or it might have called to him. But why? What was he seeking?"

"Power, no doubt," said Madame Celeste. "Or maybe it was something more personal. A vendetta, a desire for immortality, or simply the allure of the unknown. People are complex creatures, driven by myriad motivations."

"Whatever it was," Jasper continued, "it seems Leo was naturally adept. Reports from the era speak of a talent that set him apart — and eventually apart from humanity itself. He's the only spirit I've ever heard of the could take actual physical form. That must have been one heck of a spell."

"Corrupted his soul..." Nick said. Goosebumps raised on his arms, despite the warmth of the room. "Let's say he successfully cast this ultimate spell to make himself powerful after death. Is there even a way to undo something like that?"

"Undoing might not be possible," Jasper said gravely. "But containment could be within our reach. We need to identify the source of his power — the anchor that ties him to this world."

"His remains, likely," Madame Celeste posited. "It's a common thread in such tales. The physical form often holds the key."

"Then we find where he's buried," Nick said with newfound purpose, standing tall. "We find his grave, and we figure out how to break the connection."

"Easy to say," murmured Madame Celeste, her gaze

fixed on the dancing flames. "But doing so will be fraught with peril. He's not going to allow us to interfere without a fight. And remember, we have only two days remaining before he attacks. But we'll continue researching. I'm hoping one of our books will have something. I'm so glad I thought to take them with us. We also have others back in Europe scouring the Web for information."

"Either way, we'll fight," Nick declared, his jaw set. "We've got the knowledge, and we've got each other. That has to count for something."

"Indeed, it does," Jasper affirmed, closing the heavy book with a definitive thud. "Together, we'll unravel this mystery and put an end to Leo's dark legacy."

"Agreed," said Madame Celeste, rising to her feet with an elegance that belied her years. "Let us prepare, my friends. Our confrontation with Leo is inevitable, and we must be ready in body, mind, and spirit."

CHAPTER EIGHTEEN

The town square buzzed with the kind of anticipation that precedes tradition, the vibrant banners flapping like proud birds against the backdrop of a clear sky. It was Founder's Day in Gallowspine Mountains, and every soul from the surrounding county had converged to celebrate the town's storied history. Deputy Mayor Harold Jenkins stood on the bandstand, his jowls wobbling with each impassioned word.

"Esteemed citizens of Gallowspine Mountains," he bellowed, "we gather on this hallowed ground to honor the memory of our forbearers..."

Nick leaned against the trunk of an old oak, half-listening to the Deputy Mayor's speech. His mind, however, was occupied by the disturbing dreams that had haunted him for weeks, visions of shadowy figures and whispered warnings. As he scanned the crowd, his gaze fell upon familiar faces: Mrs. Whitaker from the bakery, her hands perpetually dusted with flour; Mr. Henderson, the town librarian, whose eyes squinted behind thick glasses; children darting between legs, their laughter piercing the humdrum of conversations.

"...and it is with great pride that we..." Jenkins' voice trailed off as a chill wind swept across the square. Nick shivered, the hairs on his arms standing on end. The sky darkened abruptly, a dome of rolling black clouds swallowing the sun. The crowd murmured, unsettled, searching the heavens for an explanation.

"Looks like a storm's comin'," someone muttered near Nick.

"Outta nowhere," another agreed. "Damndest thing."

Dread coiled in Nick's stomach as he watched the clouds roil and churn. A jagged bolt of lightning split the sky, striking the podium. There was an explosive crack, a blinding flash, and when the afterimage faded from Nick's vision, he saw Deputy Mayor Jenkins crumpled on the ground, smoke rising from his charred body.

It had begun.

Screams pierced the air, pandemonium erupting as the townspeople scattered in all directions. Nick stood frozen, his heart pounding — a different kind of electricity coursing through his veins. In that moment of chaos, his eyes locked onto a figure emerging from the shadows at the far end of the square.

Leo.

His presence was an omen, a harbinger of the supernatural army trailing behind him — spectral figures gliding over the cobblestones, their forms ephemeral yet terrifyingly present. The psychics had erected an invisible barrier around the square earlier that day, a safeguard against malevolent forces. But as Leo and his ghostly legion advanced, the barrier shimmered and cracked like fragile glass under a hammer's blow.

"Stand back!" one of the psychics shouted, her hands outstretched as she strained to reinforce the failing shield.

"Help the Deputy Mayor!" another cried, but it was too late; the man lay motionless, a victim not of the natural world but of the supernatural tempest that had claimed the square.

"Leo!" Nick called out, his voice steady despite the fear that clawed at his insides. The malevolent spirit turned, his eyes locking with Nick's in a silent battle of wills. Around them, the ghosts descended upon the crowd, their touch deathly cold, sowing terror and confusion.

"Nick, get down!" someone yelled, but the warning came too late. A bolt of ethereal light shot forth from Leo's outstretched hand, striking Nick squarely in the chest. He gasped, the breath knocked from his lungs, and crumpled to the ground.

The world spun, colors and sounds blending into a maelstrom. Nick fought to stay conscious, to cling to the reality that was swiftly slipping away. And then there was light, pure and blinding, engulfing him whole.

Nick's consciousness flickered, his senses numb and distant. He became aware of a gentle glow that seemed to originate from everywhere and nowhere, enveloping him in a soft radiance. It was neither warm nor cold but carried with it an undeniable sense of familiarity, as if he'd been here before, yet had no memory of it.

"Nick."

The voice cut through the thick haze, a soothing yet solemn tone that seemed to reverberate through his bones. As he blinked away the disorientation, he found himself standing in an ethereal landscape of glowing mist. Before him was a figure shrouded by the mist.

"Who are you?" Nick managed to say, his chest aching

with the phantom pain from Leo's bolt of light strike. Nick squinted through the brilliance, trying to discern the face of the man who spoke with such serene authority. As his vision adjusted, the figure before him became clearer — a robust, elderly man, age etched into his features like lines on a map, with kind eyes and a beard peppered with gray. There was an aura of wisdom about him, and a love so profound, it reached out to Nick across the impossible expanse between life and death.

"I'm Dennis Michelson, your grandfather," the man replied, a sad smile touching his lips. "I've been watching over you for a long time."

Confusion warred with recognition in Nick's mind. His grandfather had passed away when he was just a child — too young to remember the man's face, let alone his voice.

"Grandpa?" Nick echoed, disbelief tugging at the edges of his consciousness.

The figure nodded, a smile crinkling the corners of his eyes. "That's right, my boy. It's been a long time. And I'm here to help you." The man's voice was gentle, a balm to the chaos that raged within Nick. "At least, the best I can."

Nick's panicked voice echoed through the empty room. "Help me? How?" He frantically searched for any signs of life, his eyes darting around for a glimmer of hope. "Am I dead?" He finally asked, turning to his grandfather, who now appeared beside him.

"For the moment," came the stern reply. "You're in the In-Between, and we need to figure out how to get you back."

"The In-Between? I don't remember what happened."

Nick's mind whirled with thoughts, memories swirling like leaves caught in an autumn gust. How could this be happening? One moment he was in the town square, fighting for his life against an onslaught of vengeful spirits, and the next...

"Is this real?" He glanced down at his own form, ethereal and translucent against the luminous backdrop of the In-Between.

"Real is a relative term here," his grandfather replied. "But yes, this encounter holds significance."

"Are we...safe?" Nick looked around, half-expecting Leo's malevolent presence to materialize in this sanctum.

"Leo cannot reach us here, if that's what you mean. But let's not dwell on him now. This is a rare opportunity, a sliver of time outside of time."

Nick exhaled slowly, trying to anchor himself to this surreal meeting. "I don't understand why I'm here. If I'm not really dead..."

"Death isn't always permanent, especially for those whose destinies are yet unfulfilled." His grandfather's gaze was steady. "The fates have given you a chance — a pause — to gain what you need for what lies ahead."

"Which is?"

"Clarity, strength, and perhaps a little guidance." A knowing look passed over the older man's face. "You're carrying a heavy burden, Nick. The weight of countless souls."

"Those people... they didn't deserve..." Nick's voice cracked, the images of the townsfolk being struck down by spectral forces flashed through his mind.

"Many battles come with unintended casualties. Your heart knows this, even if your mind rebels against it."

"Then how do I save them? The rest of them? How do I stop all this madness?" Nick clenched his fists, feeling a surge of desperation. "How can I fight something I barely understand? Something so powerful?" The urgency was palpable in Nick's voice as he searched his grandfather's eyes for guidance. "The psychics who've come all this way to help aren't faring much better."

"Listen closely, Nick. You have a power in you, one that can turn the tide of this battle. Leo has ensnared those souls with fear, keeping them bound to his will. You need to free the ghosts from Leo's grasp. You must release them, Nick. Show them there is nothing to fear in passing on, that they can reclaim the power they've given Leo as their own. Help them find peace, and you weaken the demon."

Nick's eyes narrowed in determination. "And how do I do that? They are so many, and most of them are fighting against us."

"Reach out to them with compassion, with the under-standing that only one who has touched death can offer. Use your light to guide them to you, to break the shackles of their dread."

"Compassion," Nick echoed, the word settling into his heart like a missing puzzle piece. It made sense; if fear was the chain, then love was the key.

"Your heart, Nicholas. It's more than an organ beating in your chest; it's the conduit of your deepest connections."

"Connections..." Nick murmured, thoughts of Gabe flooding his mind. Gabe, with his unwavering loyalty and laughter that could cut through any gloom. He had to get back to Gabe, to protect him.

"Ah, you understand. Yes, by using your heart's connec-tion. The bonds you forge with others, the love that flows through you — it's more potent than you know."

"There're those words again," Nick said. "Nate thinks Gabe is my heart's connection. Is that why Gabe and I..." Nick trailed off, memories of his friend surfacing amidst the turmoil.

"Ah, yes, Gabriel. He is your anchor in this lifetime and many before. Your bond is forged not by chance, but by design. You are stronger together than apart."

"Are we...?" Nick hesitated, the revelation of past lives intertwining with the present sending a shiver through his soul.

"Your connection with Gabe is no accident. You are each other's other half, Nick. Through lifetimes, you've found one another, and now, here, you're part of something greater than yourselves. You complete each other, and your unity is essential in the battle ahead. The fate of the world rests with the two of you."

"Rests with us?" Nick said, understanding dawning within him. His responsibility in all this — his role — it was not a burden but a calling.

"Indeed. But you must trust in yourself, in your bond with Gabe, and in the light that you carry within." His grandfather's gaze pierced through Nick, instilling a sense of confidence that he desperately needed. "You and Gabe have a connection that transcends lifetimes. Use that. Let it guide you. Remember, you are each other's strength."

Nick nodded, his grandfather's words resonating deep within him. He felt a warmth spreading through his chest, a glow that suffused him with courage and resolve.

"Will we win the —?" Nick started to ask, but he already knew the answer.

"Nobody knows the outcome of this war, son. But fight with all you have and trust in Gabe. Trust in yourself."

Nick nodded, silent.

"And forgive your father," the man added, his gaze piercing. "Your path has always been set towards the light, even when shrouded in darkness. Your father... he wasn't meant to walk the same road as you. Being a medium wasn't his journey. His role was to guide you into this world, to give you life so that you could fulfill *your* destiny. And in that, he succeeded."

"Who was the entity that appeared to me?" Nick asked, seeking answers to the riddles that haunted him. "The one that paralyzed me and spoke in my mind?"

"I don't know. Some mysteries remain unsolved, even to those who dwell beyond life's veil." He laughed. "Hell, most of them do."

"But can we stop Leo?" Nick's voice trembled with urgency.

"Nobody knows, Nick. But give it your best and let Gabe help you. Together, you stand a chance. Remember, you are more powerful together than you are individually."

"Clear!" a strange voice rang out.

And with a sudden rush that felt like being pulled through a vortex, Nick's consciousness catapulted back to the town square in Gallowspine Mountains.

CHAPTER NINETEEN

Nick lay prone, his body a mere husk against the icy embrace of the hard stones. A ring of faces hovered above, their expressions a reflection of fear, hope, and disbelief. Among them was Scott, the paramedic whose hands were fervently working over Nick's still form.

"Charge to 300!" Scott barked, his voice betraying none of the dread that clawed at his insides. The defibrillator whined, a harbinger of pain or salvation — only fate would decide which.

"Clear!" he shouted, and the world seemed to contract into the space between Nick's chest and the hovering paddles.

The electricity surged, a violent force jolting through Nick's body, causing it to arch like a bowstring pulled taut. Then silence — heavy, thick, oppressive silence.

Scott leaned over, his ear close to Nick's mouth, eyes flicking to the second hand of his watch. Seconds crawled by, each one an eternity unto itself.

And then, a miracle breathed into being.

"He's alive," someone said, the words spreading through the crowd like the first rays of dawn after an endless night.

Gabe, who had been standing silently, fists clenched with powerless rage, felt his knees buckle. Tears flowed unbidden down his cheeks. For over two minutes — two lifetimes — he had thought his boyfriend gone, taken by the darkness they had vowed to fight together.

"Nick?" Gabe choked out, his voice a raw whisper carrying all the weight of his grief turned to sudden, fragile hope.

Nick's eyelids fluttered open, his gaze unfocused but unmistakably alive. His chest heaved in a ragged gasp, drawing in the cool evening air as if it were the sweetest nectar. He coughed, a sound more beautiful than any symphony to those who kept the silent vigil.

"Scott?" Nick's voice was barely audible.

"Right here, buddy. You gave us quite the scare," Scott replied, his steady hands now resting lightly on Nick's shoulder, grounding him to the here and now. "Someone said they saw you get struck by lightning. We're lucky you're still with us." Scott looked around him. "I don't understand what's happening here. Where are these bolts of lightening coming from? It looks like they're coming from the ground instead of the sky. I've never seen any storm like this one."

"Water..." Nick's throat was a desert, each word a sand-storm scratching its way out.

"Right here," Scott said.

"Nick, do you know where you are?" Scott continued, professional concern etched into his brow.

"Town... square," Nick managed, his mind clawing back from the abyss that had claimed him. Memories swirled like leaves in an autumn gale, sharp and fragmented. He then became aware of the chaos of the battle, the cries of the townsfolk, the wails of the ensnared spirits, and the oppressive might of the storm clouds above. A bolt of lightning seared the ground mere feet away, its crackling energy a reminder of the deadly dance unfolding around him.

"Take it easy," Scott soothed, ignoring the chaos all around them. "You've been out for a bit."

"Out?" Nick echoed, struggling to piece together the shards of time he'd lost.

"Over two minutes, man," Gabe interjected, his voice thick with emotion. "You were dead." The tears he'd tried to stem flowed freely now, carving clear paths through the grime on his face.

"Two minutes?" Nick repeated, disbelief coloring his tone. Inside, a storm brewed; thoughts crashed against each other, vying for dominance. Had he truly died?

"Seems like longer," Nick murmured, wincing as he tried to push himself up. His muscles protested, pain flaring across every nerve ending.

Lurching upright, Nick noticed the residual ache in his chest from the shafts of light that had struck him down. Through the haze, he saw the psychics, arms raised, doing their best to protect the town.

"Whoa there, tiger, easy does it," Scott cautioned, gently pressing him back down. "You took a nasty hit. We need to make sure everything's in working order before you go playing hero again." He looked around him.

"Can't... stay down," Nick rasped, determination seeping into his voice. The battle — their cause — it wasn't over. Not by a long shot.

"Nick, you're back!" Maya cried out, rushing up to them. "Thank God."

"Wouldn't miss this for the world," Nick replied, his

voice steady despite the thunderous heartbeat in his ears. "Where's Leo?" The name left his lips before he fully grasped the weight of it, the urgency propelling him to sit up again, this time with success.

"The others are holding him back for now, but they're weakening fast." Maya glanced over her shoulder, where across the square, a group of individuals shrouded in iridescent shields were barely containing a figure radiating malevolence. "Let's hope Jasper is successful."

"Jasper?" Nick asked, trying to remember. His thoughts were so muddled.

"He thinks he found out where Leo is buried and is on his way there to do a ritual and then destroy the remains. Madame Celeste believes that if we destroy his remains, it should break his bond with the living world and the spell that allows him to take physical form." She clenched her fists. "I don't know what else we can do. It looks like all is lost."

"Like hell it is," Nick said, determination infusing his voice. He swung his legs off the makeshift stretcher and onto the ground, the coolness of the cobbles seeping through his boots. Every muscle protested, but he ignored the pain. He reached out, grabbing Gabe's hands, feeling an inexplicable warmth spread from the point of contact.

"Nick! What are you —" Scott began, but stopped short as the light enveloped both Nick and Gabe.

"Nick, you can't!" Gabe protested, reaching out to steady him. "You've barely come back from —"

"From death," Nick finished for him, his voice a low growl of defiance. "And if I can come back from that, then we can come back from this." Struggling to his feet, Nick felt the familiar thrum of connection with Gabe, a lifeline amidst the tempest. They locked eyes, and without a word, they understood each other.

"Damn right we can," Gabe said, his resolve returning. Together, they advanced toward the fray, moving as one.

"Leo won't win," Nick declared, the fire within him blazing brighter with every step. "We'll make damn sure of it."

"But Nick, we sure could use a miracle," Gabe said, his hand gripping Nick's arm. "Something... anything."

Nick sucked in a deep breath. Wasn't his very existence at this moment a miracle? The line between possible and impossible had blurred the moment he'd drawn a breath again.

"How about we make our own miracle?" Nick said, a surge of adrenaline lending strength to his voice.

Nick raised his hands before him, not knowing what he expected to happen, only that he must try. He reached out with his newly understood power, extending tendrils of light towards the tormented ghosts. He whispered words of solace and freedom, each syllable laced with the essence of his heart's connection.

"Gabe, focus on the ghosts," Nick said, reaching out with his senses to touch the ethereal forms swirling around them. He remembered his grandfather's advice — to use his heart's connection. He closed his eyes for a moment, centering himself, finding that deep well of empathy within. "We have to convince them to let go of their guilt and fear. That's the key."

"Spirits, free yourselves from him!" Nick shouted, his voice carrying over the battlefield. "You don't have to be bound by fear!"

Gabe was beside him, his presence radiating warmth

and light. Together, they stood firm, their combined strength a bulwark against the encroaching shadows.

"Remember who you were!" Gabe implored the ghosts, his tone a blend of command and compassion. A few of the spirits hesitated, their forms becoming less opaque, the hold of fear loosening.

"Look forward, not back," Nick added, reinforcing Gabe's call. He watched as some of the ghosts began to disentangle themselves from Leo's grasp, their expressions softening with the realization of their own agency. "There's peace and freedom for you in the light."

Ghosts hesitated, flickers of clarity appearing in their hollow eyes as the strength of Nick's conviction began to erode Leo's hold.

"Keep going, Nick!" Gabe shouted, gripping Nick's shoulder firmly. "It's working! They're listening to you!"

At Gabe's touch, a blast of strength and power surged through him. "Right," Nick agreed, refocusing on the present. He grabbed Gabe's hand and intertwined their fingers. His grandfather's words echoed in his mind. "We're stronger together."

"Listen to me!" Nick shouted, tapping into the newfound clarity bestowed upon him by his grandfather's wisdom. "Your fear is Leo's chain! Break free!"

"Think of your loved ones waiting for you!" Gabe added, his voice echoing Nick's plea.

One by one, the spirits paused, turning their hollow gazes towards Nick and Gabe. A ghostly woman, her translucent hand hovering over her heart, nodded slowly before dissolving into a wisp of light, her essence ascending towards the heavens.

Gabe and Nick moved as one, their unity emboldening those around them. With every pushback against Leo's forces, the balance shifted, hope weaving its way through the despair.

Then a ghost, its form flickering like a faulty lamp, lunged towards Nick with a wail that cut through the din of the battle. The specter was draped in remnants of a past life — a soldier from a forgotten war, perhaps, carrying the echo of old orders and the weight of eternal regret.

"Stop!" Nick commanded, his hand raised as if to shield himself. Yet instead of contact, there was an explosion of light from his palm, an ethereal force that enveloped the attacking ghost. "Forget your fear," Nick urged, his voice surprisingly gentle. "Find peace."

"The light, it's so beautiful," the ghost murmured, his corporeal struggles ceasing as he beheld the light that bathed him. And then, with a sigh of relief, he walked right through Nick and vanished into nothingness.

Nick staggered slightly, gasping as the ghost's entire life flashed inside of Nick's mind in a series of vivid snapshots: a childhood spent running through fields, laughter around a family table, the horror of battlefields, and finally, the unending limbo of the afterlife. Empathy for the ghost's plight settled deep within Nick's heart.

"Are you okay?" Gabe asked, concern lacing his words as he steadied Nick.

"More than okay," Nick replied, though his voice was distant, still resonating with the echo of the life he'd just witnessed. A new realization took hold of him. "I'm what they need."

As if drawn by a clarion call, more ghosts converged on him. They were a motley crew, each tethered to the earthly plane for different reasons. One by one, Nick spoke to them, his words a balm to their unrest.

"Release your chains," he said to a woman, her eyes

hollow with decades of watching the world change without her. "It's time to be free." She nodded, a gesture of gratitude, and then she too passed through him, leaving a trace of her essence behind — memories of whispered secrets and moonlit rendezvous.

"Let go of your anger," he implored a young man consumed by a fiery aura of vengeance, his fists still clenched in defiance. It took mere moments for the fury to dissolve, replaced by understanding, and then liberation as he crossed the threshold of Nick's being.

Each encounter was a revelation. The spirits flowed into Nick like tributaries joining a great river, their collective histories merging with his own. There was no fear in their passage, only release, and as they departed, it was as if they left fragments of their souls with him, pieces of a puzzle he was only just beginning to understand.

"Nick, how are you doing this?" Gabe's inquiry was tinged with amazement. Around them, the psychics continued their struggle, their voices a chorus against the encroaching darkness.

"I don't know," Nick admitted, his voice barely louder than a whisper.

"Whatever it is, keep going," Gabe encouraged, his grip on Nick's hand unwavering. "It's working. You're releasing them."

And Nick did continue, bolstered by Gabe's support. More spirits came, each with their own stories etched into their essence. A mother who had lost her child, a poet whose words had never seen the light of day, an old man who simply missed the sun on his face. All found solace in Nick's light, all stepped through the veil and into peace.

"Thank you," they whispered in unison, their voices like

a breeze that stirred the leaves of the trees lining the square, their gratitude imprinting itself upon Nick's soul.

As more spirits lined up, drawn to him like moths to a flame, Nick experienced the weight of their stories, their regrets, and their desires to move on. His body thrummed with energy, each crossing leaving him both drained and strangely replenished.

Another ghost interrupted his thoughts, this one a young woman who clutched a locket close to her chest. Her eyes held years of sorrow, and as she passed through Nick, the sting of her tears, the sharp pang of lost love flowed through him.

"Thank you," she whispered, her presence fading within him.

"Keep going," Nick whispered to himself, his focus narrowing as he became a conduit for redemption. "Just keep going."

A spectral figure approached, its ethereal form flickering with uncertainty. The ghost's fear became Nick's fear, a palpable thing that strummed against his senses. With a gentle movement, he extended his hand, palm glowing with an incandescent warmth. "Don't be afraid," he urged softly. The ghost hesitated, then reached forward, its hand disappearing into the light that enveloped Nick. A sense of relief washed over the spirit's face, and with a grateful nod, it stepped forward and melded into Nick's form. There was a momentary flash, and the ghost was gone.

"Look! Nick is the light," Eliza exclaimed from the periphery of the scene, her voice carrying over the tumult with urgency. She pointed at Nick with a trembling hand, her eyes wide with revelation. "Ghosts are crossing over through him!"

"Remarkable," Nate murmured, his eyes never leaving

Nick. "He's not just guiding them... He's becoming their passage. He's an extension of the light."

"Is it safe for him?" Raphael asked from within the circle that had formed around Nick, concern etched into her furrowed brow. They all watched, transfixed by the spectacle unfolding before them.

"I don't know," Nate replied, his lips pressed into a thin line. "Let's hope so. Because safe or not, it's necessary. Without him, the balance tips in favor of despair."

"Are you holding up okay?" Gabe squeezed Nick's hand tighter, grounding him.

"I see all of their lives," Nick confessed, his voice a mere breath. "It's damned exhausting. But I have to keep going. For them. For everyone."

One by one, the ghosts came. Each crossing was a story, a life, a last goodbye. And Nick, bathed in a light that was both end and beginning.

"Keep pushing through," Nate encouraged, his earlier skepticism replaced with respect. "You are the bridge, Nick. You're what they've been waiting for."

"Let's hope it's enough," Nick thought, steeling himself for the next spirit, his heart echoing with the weight of his new duty.

"Nick, look out!" Gabe's voice cut through the din as a vast tide of ghosts, their forms shimmering like heat haze, surged toward them. There was no time for thought, only reaction, as Nick extended his hands, palms outward, bracing for the impact.

"Let them come," he whispered, more to himself than to Gabe. The pull of the beyond was stronger now, a vortex centered in the core of his being. Nick felt it. Another spirit reached him — a woman whose eyes held the weight of unspent years — and passed through him without resistance. Her life, her regrets, all flickered within Nick's mind for a fleeting moment before she was gone, leaving an aching hollow in her wake. Nick stumbled, now unsteady on his feet. He was weakening.

"I don't know how much longer I can do this," Nick said. Each ghost carried a cacophony of emotions, a fragment of the life they once lived, threatening to drown Nick in a deluge of their collective pasts.

"Stay with me, dude." Gabe's fingers laced through his, a lifeline anchoring him to the present as the onslaught continued.

"Can't... It's too much," Nick gasped. His knees buckled under the sheer volume of souls passing through him. His vision blurred, edges fraying into darkness as he struggled to remain conscious.

"Focus on my voice," Gabe urged, his presence a constant amidst the chaos. "I'm right here, lending you my strength. You can do this." Gabe squeezed his hand tighter and grasped Nick's shoulder with his other hand.

Energy surged into Nick — energy given to him by Gabe. He straightened and took a deep breath. Then another. "I'm better."

One by one, the ghosts dissipated, their chains of fear dissolving into motes of light that ascended skyward. Leo's army diminished, his control wavering as Nick and Gabe stood united, a beacon of defiance amidst the darkness.

The battle raged on, but with each freed spirit, the tide turned ever so slightly in their favor. Nick knew that no matter the outcome, he would fight until the very end, with his heart, his connection, and Gabe at his side.

"Liars! Deceivers!" Leo's voice boomed across the square, laced with panic and fury. His once-mighty army dwindled with each spirit that crossed through Nick rather than fight. "You dare betray me for this false shepherd? The light will burn you, flay your souls! Eternal torment, that's what awaits you."

Nick's response rose from within, a deep, resounding timbre that filled the space between heartbeats and breaths. "There's no pain where you're going," he called out, his voice somehow cutting through the tumult. "Only release from fear. From torment."

"Your insolence will be the end of you!" Leo seethed, and as if in response to his rage, the ground trembled. It began as a subtle vibration, but quickly escalated into a violent quake that sent people sprawling. Screams pierced the air as the townsfolk scrambled for safety, terror lending speed to their steps. They all looked dazed, eyes blank, as if their brains had shut down and their bodies moved now on autopilot.

"Watch out!" Nate yelled as the towering statue of the town's founder shuddered ominously.

"Kids! Get away from there!" Nick's warning came as the statue's base cracked, chunks of rock tumbling down like the first ominous raindrops of a storm.

"Nick!" Gabe's voice was a blend of alarm and determination. "The children!"

Time slowed for Nick. With every ounce of his newfound strength, he sprinted toward the group of five kids who stood frozen beneath the teetering statue. Confusion and fear painted their faces, eyes wide and uncomprehending of the danger they were in.

"Move!" Nick's command was more forceful than he'd ever heard it, propelled by the urgency of the moment. He lunged forward, arms outstretched, his entire being focused on the lives he was desperate to save.

"Mommy!" One little girl's cry was nearly lost amidst

the cacophony, but it was enough to spur her legs into motion, mirroring the rush of her companions as they scattered.

Nick's dive carried him through the air, his hands grazing the backs of the last two children as he pushed them clear. They stumbled away, tumbling over one another in their haste. The massive shadow of the teetering falling statue loomed over them.

"Gotcha!" Nick's exclamation was more of a grunt than a word as his body collided with the cold, hard ground, the impact jarring his bones. He rolled, tucking his head, instinctively shielding his face from the debris that rained down as the statue smashed to the ground next to them, where the children had stood only a moment before.

"Is everyone okay?" Nick's voice was ragged as he pulled himself up, scanning for the children. His heart thundered against his ribs, each beat a prayer that he had been fast enough.

"Nick, that was... You just..." Gabe stammered, words failing him as relief washed over his features. "I thought we were going to lose them."

"Me too," Nick admitted, his throat tight. He looked at the rubble where the statue once stood, now a testament to the narrow escape. "But we didn't. That's what matters."

"Nick, look!" Nate pointed back to where the spectral conflict had raged. Leo's apparition was nowhere to be seen, but the remnants of his influence still lingered. Ghosts hovered uncertainly, drawn to Nick, yet fearful of their malevolent leader's warnings.

"Come on," Nick beckoned, his resolve firming. "It's time to finish what we started."

The tremors underfoot had ceased, leaving behind an eerie silence that blanketed the town square. Nick stood, his chest heaving with exertion and eyes ablaze with celestial fire. The ghosts that had lingered uncertainly now thronged around him, their ephemeral forms wavering like candle flames in a storm.

"Take my hand again," he told Gabe, breathless from the exertion.

As soon as their palms met, the light enveloped them once more, a tangible force of protection and potency. They turned to face Leo, who hovered above the square, disdain written across his features.

"Look at you, playing savior!" Leo's scornful voice cut through the serene moment, ripe with contempt. His figure levitated above the ground, dark energy swirling like a storm cloud ready to burst. "Now Nick Michelson, you die!"

Nick felt the words before he heard them, a premonition chilling him to the core. Leo's hands crackled with power as he conjured two bolts of searing light, aiming them with lethal precision at Nick's heart.

Time slowed, or so it seemed to Nick. He could see the minute particles of dust caught in the radiant trajectory of the deadly beams. And yet, there was no fear in his heart — only resolve. With Gabe's support, Nick felt invincible, not because of any delusion of grandeur, but because he knew they stood for something greater than themselves.

As the bolts hurtled towards them, that same unshakeable calm took hold of Nick, as he knew exactly what to do. Without hesitation, he thrust their conjoined hands forward, a shield made not of flesh and bone, but of pure, unadulterated light.

The impact was less a collision and more of an explosion — the sound of darkness breaking against an impenetrable wall of radiance. The bolts of light fractured, splintering into countless shards that recoiled back towards their originator.

"Impossible!" Leo's snarl was the last word he said before the refracted light struck him squarely in the chest. But it seemed to have little effect on him.

Suddenly, Leo looked skyward, as though something had caught his attention. "What? No!" His scream pierced the air, a sound so full of anguish and disbelief that it resonated in Nick's very soul. "It can't be!"

Leo's body became a silhouette against the brilliance, his edges fraying like paper licked by flame. Then, with a final, anguished cry that echoed off the stone buildings surrounding the square, he exploded into a fiery inferno that consumed him wholly. Nothing remained of the tyrant, not even ash — only the lingering echoes of his demise.

"Did we... Did we just win?" Gabe's voice trembled, a mix of hope and incredulity.

"I think we did." Nick's gaze swept across the sea of faces — both living and dead — that surrounded them, all transfixed by the spectacle they had witnessed. "But how? He just disappeared."

"More like blew up," Gabe said.

Everyone's phone beeped at once. "It's a text from Jasper," Nate said. "He has just finished burning Leo's remains."

"Nick." Gabe's grip tightened, grounding him. "You're glowing."

"Am I?" For the first time since the ordeal began, a laugh escaped Nick's lips — a sound that seemed foreign in the aftermath of battle. "Then let's make sure this light leads everyone home."

And so they stood, side by side, as the bridge and the guardian. The departed continued to come, one by one, each crossing through Nick until the square grew empty, and the night reclaimed its stillness. Gabe held on tight to Nick's hand. The overwhelming tide became a stream, then a trickle, until silence settled over the square once more. Somehow, Gabe provided him with the strength to continue.

"Nick..." The voice was a whisper wrapped in warmth, and with it came the familiar scent of sandalwood and cedar — the cologne that Uncle Mitch had worn like a signature. "You're doing it. You're freeing them all."

Uncle Mitch materialized, his spectral form more solid than the other. His eyes, mirroring Nick's own, held a mixture of pride and sorrow.

"Uncle Mitch..." Nick breathed. Tears flooded his eyes. "How —"

"Leo," Mitch said, his gaze sweeping over the dissipating spirits. "He trapped us here, fed on our fear because we wouldn't join him, wouldn't surrender to his reign of terror. But you, Nick, you've broken his hold."

"Me?" Doubt laced Nick's thoughts, even as his uncle's words bolstered him. "I'm just... I don't understand how I did it."

"Ah, but you are something rare, Nick. You're a reaper." Uncle Mitch's voice held reverence, a note of awe. "I'd heard tales of your kind over the years, but to see it, to see you — it's more than I ever imagined."

"Reaper..." The word echoed in Nick's skull, resonating with a truth he'd never known yet always felt. The spirits weren't just passing through him; they were finding solace, release. "Is that why this is happening?"

"Because you are the bridge between worlds," Mitch confirmed. "You guide them to peace."

"The concept settled into Nick's bones. It wasn't just

about fighting, about the clash of light and shadow. It was about resolution, about ushering these souls to a rest that Leo had denied them.

"Your light, it frightened Leo," Mitch continued, his figure beginning to fade. "It's purity he couldn't corrupt, courage he couldn't quell. You've saved us all."

Nick gestured his head toward Gabe. "*We* saved them."

"It's time for me to finally move on," Uncle Mitch said, his voice steady yet tinged with an emotion that Nick couldn't quite name. "May I cross through you?"

Nick nodded before the words even left his lips. "It would be my honor, Uncle Mitch."

Mitch stepped closer, and for a fleeting moment, Nick wanted to reach out, to touch the man who had been more father than uncle, to assure himself that this last farewell was real.

"Thank you," Mitch whispered, raising a hand that shimmered with the same light that had enveloped Nick when he'd faced the ghosts. "For everything, for being brave enough to accept who you are."

Nick's throat tightened, the weight of the gift — and the curse — of being a reaper pressing upon him like the gravity of a thousand worlds. He swallowed hard, his heart a drumbeat echoing in the emptiness.

"Uncle Mitch, I —" but the words lodged there, a knot of gratitude and fear.

"Shhh." Uncle Mitch smiled, a gentle curve of his lips that pulled at memories of laughter and lessons learned beneath the shade of old oaks. "You're ready for this, Nick. You always have been."

With each word, Nick's resolve solidified like ice over a wintry lake. He was ready. He had to be. Every soul he'd helped across tonight proved that much, even if doubt still clawed at the edges of his mind.

"Take care of Gabe," Mitch said, his eyes flickering to where Gabe stood a few paces away, a sentinel of strength and solace. "And tell him...thank you."

"I will," Nick promised, and the words were a vow etched into the marrow of his bones.

Mitch nodded and took the ultimate step, closing the distance between them. As he passed through Nick, there was a sensation unlike any other — a warmth that suffused every cell.

Nick closed his eyes, letting the tears fall, because with Uncle Mitch's crossing, a part of him went too — a part that had been safe and cherished and known. When he opened them again, Mitch was gone, but the light remained, a soft glow that lingered in the space between heartbeats.

"Goodbye," Nick whispered to the night, to the stars, to the man who had shown him what it meant to live and now what it meant to let go.

Gabe moved to his side, a look of concern on his face. "Nick, are you okay?"

"Uncle Mitch just crossed through me," Nick said, his voice low, the words seeming strange and surreal. "He's gone, Gabe. He's really gone."

"I know," Gabe replied, his hand finding Nick's shoulder, a point of contact that kept Nick anchored to the here and now. "But you did it. You led him and all the others home."

Home was where the heart was, they said, and now pieces of Nick's heart stretched far beyond the veil, carried within the souls who'd crossed through him.

"Nick?" Gabe's voice cut through the stillness, tentative

yet filled with an undercurrent of awe. "You did it. I mean… you actually did it."

A nod was all Nick could manage, the gravity of his newfound purpose weighing heavily upon him.

"Did it hurt?" Gabe asked, stepping closer, his eyes searching Nick's face for signs of strain.

"In a way, yes," Nick admitted, his words barely above a breath. The physical toll was nothing compared to the emotional onslaught — the stories, the regrets, the loves and losses of so many now etched within him.

"God, I can't even begin to understand." Gabe shook his head.

"Yeah, me neither."

"Look at you," Gabe murmured, reaching out to trace the fading light that hugged Nick's frame, "like some kind of beacon."

"Beacon or reaper," Nick mused, a wry smile tugging at the corner of his mouth despite the somber mood. "I have a feeling that my life has just taken a new turn in a direction I never expected."

"Does anyone ever really expect the way their lives turn out?" Gabe countered, his hand dropping to his side. "But you're embracing it, dude. That's what matters."

"Embracing it? Ha! It's more like I'm being dragged along for the ride, all the while kicking and screaming," Nick half-joked, allowing a momentary laugh to bubble up from the well of emotions swirling inside him.

"Maybe so," Gabe conceded, "but you're steering the ship now. Wherever we're headed, I trust you at the helm."

"So what's with the ship metaphors?"

Gabe shrugged and chuckled. "I dunno, but they kinda work, don't they?"

The air quivered with the energy of a storm spent, the

last remnants of an otherworldly storm fading into the night. The town square, once alight with the battle and the cries of the living and dead alike, had grown eerily silent, save for the soft rustle of leaves. Thankfully, most of the townspeople had fled the square early on. The casualties could have been much worse.

Nick and Gabe joined the other psychics near the overturned vendor booths and they all moved together through the square, past the shattered statue that had nearly claimed innocent lives, toward a horizon tinged with the promise of dawn. And as they went, the lingering scent of cologne, Uncle Mitch's cologne, followed Nick, a reminder that while some journeys end, others are just beginning.

CHAPTER TWENTY

THE SQUARE WAS AWASH WITH THE GOLDEN HUES OF AN autumn day, leaves falling like slow embers from the trees that lined the cobblestone paths. A gentle breeze carried the scent of cider and cinnamon from nearby vendors, mingling with the soft murmur of townsfolk gathering in the heart of the town, eyes bright with pride and curiosity.

At the center of it all stood Nick, alone amidst the crowd, overcome by waves of bittersweet emotions. The medal they were about to hang around his neck felt undeserved, heavy with a weight he wasn't sure he could bear. He scanned the faces in the crowd, recognizing neighbors, friends, and strangers — all of whom looked at him as if he were a hero.

"Nick Michelson!" Mayor Samuelson's voice boomed across the square as he beckoned Nick forward. "Step up, son!"

Nick moved as if in a dream, his feet knowing the way better than his distracted mind. He ascended the small platform erected for the ceremony, the wood creaking underfoot.

"Today, we honor Nicholas Michelson," the mayor continued, his chest puffed out like a proud pigeon, "for his bravery in saving our children from certain peril." Applause erupted, a wave of sound that washed over Nick, making his ears ring. The mayor lifted the gleaming medal, catching the sunlight, and draped it over Nick's head.

Nick smiled sheepishly as the medal settled heavily around his neck. The metal was cool against his skin, a stark contrast to the warm sun beaming down on the crowded town square. Cameras flashed from the crowd, capturing every moment of his awkward bashfulness.

"As a token of our community's gratitude," the mayor boomed, gesturing towards a table laden with more symbols of recognition, "we also present you with this certificate of valor and a scholarship to support your future endeavors, ensuring that your courage and selflessness are not only remembered but rewarded."

Whispers of admiration swirled through the crowd as Nick approached the table, his eyes widening slightly at the sight of the official-looking documents and a check bearing his name.

Nick took a moment to absorb the scene before him — the smiling faces, the colorful banners fluttering in the breeze, and the sense of community unity. It felt surreal, a stark departure from the chaos and fear of that fateful day when he had acted not out of heroism, but necessity. Yet, here he was, being celebrated as a hero.

The mayor clasped his shoulder, bringing him back to the moment. "Nicholas, would you like to say a few words?" he asked, handing him the microphone.

Nick hesitated, the weight of the crowd's expectations pressing down on him. But as he looked out over the sea of encouraging faces, he found his resolve. Clearing his throat, he began to speak, his voice steady but humble, "Thank you, everyone. I did what anyone else would do in my place. I'm just glad I could help, and that everyone is safe. That's the most important thing to me." His words, simple and sincere, earned him another round of heartfelt applause as the community celebrated not just the act of bravery, but the unassuming bravery of one of their own.

The crowd cheered again, but their cheers couldn't drown out the thunderous silence that resounded within him — the absence of his uncle's voice, who would have been his loudest supporter.

"You're a hero, son," the mayor exclaimed, placing a heavy hand on Nick's shoulder. As everyone gathered around to praise him, Nick couldn't help but experience a twinge of unease. How did they not remember what really happened that day? His eyes scanned the crowd. Even now, nobody was sure what truly occurred during those chaotic moments. All they agreed on was that Nicholas Michelson was at the center of it all and that more people would have perished if it wasn't for him.

"Thank you, sir," Nick repeated mechanically.

As the applause died down, Nick's eyes scanned the crowd and caught sight of a familiar face. There was Quinn, leaning against an old bur oak tree.

"Congratulations, kiddo," Quinn said with a ghostly grin as Nick approached. "They're right, you know. You really are a hero."

Quinn's translucent form wavered, and a melancholic sigh seemed to echo through the air. The ethereal glow that surrounded him dimmed as guilt clouded his ghostly countenance.

"Nick," Quinn murmured, his voice carrying a weight

heavy with remorse. "I need to tell you something, something that I've been hiding from you. Something I'm deeply ashamed of but something you need to know." His incorporeal figure flickered like a dying flame as he continued, "It was me. I'm the one who told Leo where to find your Uncle Mitch. I betrayed your uncle."

The words hung in the air, mingling with the quiet whispers of the wind. Nick's smile faded, replaced by a mixture of confusion and disbelief. His heart raced, searching for answers amidst the storm of emotions.

"Why, Quinn? Why would you do such a thing?" Nick's voice quivered with both anger and anguish. Every cell in his body ached with betrayal, his mind struggling to comprehend the magnitude of Quinn's confession.

Quinn's ghostly form trembled as he met Nick's gaze, the guilt in his eyes mirroring the pain etched on Nick's face. "I did it out of fear, Nick," he confessed, his voice barely a whisper against the autumn breeze. "Leo threatened me. He said he would destroy everything I held dear if I didn't help him."

Nick's fists clenched at his sides, his knuckles turning white as anger surged through his veins. "You killed my Uncle Mitch!" he spat, unable to contain the fury that consumed him. The weight of the medal around his neck suddenly seemed to suffocate him.

Quinn lowered his gaze, unable to meet Nick's accusing stare. "I realize what I did was unforgivable. But please understand, Nick, I never wanted any harm to come to your uncle or to anyone else. Leo's influence was overpowering, and I couldn't escape it. He threatened to kill my family and I think he would have, too."

Nick's anger subsided as quickly as it had risen, seeping

away like the last rays of sunlight at dusk. The weight of betrayal still lingered, but so did a flicker of empathy for Quinn. Nick might have done the same thing under similar circumstances. Nick would do anything to protect those he loved.

"Quinn," Nick said, his voice softened with a mixture of sadness and forgiveness. "I can't pretend that what you did doesn't hurt, but I also understand that fear can drive people to do terrible things." He paused for a moment, gathering his thoughts.

"Tell me again how you met Leo," Nick asked, trying to distract himself from the grief that threatened to overwhelm him.

Quinn's form flickered as he spoke, memories flooding back from a time long gone. "I met him when I was still alive. He... he had a way of convincing people. Made me believe he was a psychic, too. He told me he wanted to meet other fellow psychics and learn from them." A hint of bitterness crept into Quinn's voice as he continued, "That's how he got me to spill about Mitch. Your uncle and I were friends, you know? I was also a psychic when I was alive, though not a medium like the two of you. I worked the fair and carnival circuit for a couple of years and your uncle and I ran in the same circles for a bit. He was one of the nicest people I've ever met and took me under his wing. Anyway, one day Leo showed up and befriended me. I had no idea what he really was, that he wasn't even human. He got me to trust him. And then..."

"And then he killed you," Nick finished for him, anger and sadness warring within him.

But as they stood there in silence, staring at each other with understanding and regret, Nick couldn't help but feel grateful for the short friendship with Quinn. Without him, he may have never discovered the truth about Leo and finally put an end to his reign of terror.

"Yep. And then he went after Mitch," Quinn said, his gaze dropping to the spectral hands he turned over and over before him. "I led him right there. I feel responsible for his and my deaths."

"Quinn, listen to me," Nick said firmly, laying a hand on Quinn's cold, insubstantial shoulder. "Uncle Mitch crossed over. He told me everything that happened was supposed to happen."

"Supposed to?" Quinn echoed hollowly, a shimmer passing through him like a ripple over water.

"Your death, my learning curve, my uncle's guidance — it was all part of something bigger." Nick explained, his throat tightening as he uttered the words.

"Your uncle, he was fully aware of what he was doing. Training you," Quinn said, his eyes lifting to meet Nick's. "You think I can... cross over now?"

"I think so," Nick said. "You can let go of the guilt. You're free."

"Thank you, Nick," Quinn murmured, and as he faded into Nick, Nick saw flashes of Quinn's life — the good times, the bad, moments of joy and despair — all the things that made him human.

And then Quinn was gone, leaving Nick alone with the echo of his own heartbeat and the realization that nothing would ever be the same. Tomorrow, he would walk back into school, back to normalcy, or the closest semblance of it. How strange it would be to sit in class, to walk the halls, surrounded by the oblivious rhythm of teenage life.

"Nick?" a voice called, pulling him from his reverie. It was Mrs. Dalrymple, his English teacher. "Are you alright, dear?"

"Y-yeah, just... thinking," Nick stammered, forcing a smile.

"It's all quite overwhelming, isn't it?" she said kindly, patting his arm. "But understand that the entire town is proud of you." She smiled and then moved away, leaving Nick to stand in the fading light.

As Nick watched Mrs. Dalrymple walk away, a weight lifted off his chest. Sure, Quinn's confession had shaken him, but he had found solace because it was all part of a larger plan. Uncle Mitch had always been there to guide him, even from beyond the grave.

Nick returned to the chaos of the crowd, still buzzing with excitement. The admiration and applause they offered him felt hollow now, but he appreciated the sentiment. He had been a hero, and now he understood the true cost of that label.

As the sun began to set, Nick took a deep breath and plunged back into the crowd. He would face the remaining days of high school, his heart heavy with the knowledge of what truly transpired. He would carry the memory of his uncle with him, as well as the memory of Quinn, and the countless others who had come and gone in his life.

School resumed the next day, after a several day hiatus to honor the fallen. Nick returned to Gallowspine High and as he walked through the halls, he couldn't help but feel like a different person. The hustle and bustle of high school life seemed almost surreal compared to the otherworldly experiences he had just endured. He walked past lockers adorned with pictures of pop stars and sports teams, past walls covered in school spirit posters and announcements for weekend parties. There were also memorialized lockers belonging to students who'd perished during Leo's attack.

He made his way to his first class, and as he took his

seat, he noticed that everyone around him seemed preoccupied with their phones and headphones. Nobody seemed to acknowledge the strange events that had occurred a mere few days ago. It was as if nobody remembered what had happened in the square, only that there was pandemonium and people had died. Many blamed it on a freak storm. Some claimed an earthquake. Maybe they were scared, or maybe they simply wanted to pretend it hand't happened

It was as if the world had moved on, and in a way, Nick was grateful for that. The last time he spoke with Katrina, she had told him that people forget on purpose. It's their subconscious way of dealing with situations that don't make sense or that they don't understand. It's easier just to forget.

That evening, Nick returned home to a house filled with the warmth and familiarity of his family. The comforting aroma of his mother's homemade cooking greeted him at the door, while the sound of his father's favorite jazz recording floated through the air. It was a scene that had played out countless times before, but tonight, there was an underlying excitement that crackled beneath the surface.

As Nick entered the living room, he found his parents sitting on the couch, his dad engrossed in a book and his mom, a crossword puzzle. On the other side of the room, his younger sister Missy sat at her desk, her brow furrowed in concentration as she scribbled away in her sketchbook. They were all so absorbed in their own worlds that they hadn't noticed Nick's arrival.

"Hey guys," Nick called out, breaking their reverie. Instantly, their attention shifted to him, their faces lighting up with smiles.

"Nick! You're home!" his mother exclaimed, setting

aside her book and rushing to embrace him. "We've missed you."

"I missed you all too," Nick replied, hugging his mother tightly. A rush of gratitude for the love and support that surrounded him surged through him.

"Are the psychics still here?" his mother asked.

Nick shook his head. "They left two days ago. They all waited until Sia was released from the hospital. Luckily, she ended up only with a broken arm and some bruises. So when did you all get home?"

"About noon," his mother said. "Your auntie sends her love, by the way."

His father looked up from his crossword puzzle, a twinkle in his eyes. "So, son, how does it feel to be a hero?"

Nick chuckled, sliding into the vacant spot beside his father on the couch. "It's strange, Dad. At school today, everyone acted like nothing had happened. It was the weirdest thing. It's like everyone's got amnesia."

His sister Missy joined them, her face alive with curiosity. "So, tell us everything, Nick! We want to hear all the details about how you saved the world."

Nick looked at his sister, the way her eyes sparkled with anticipation. Missy had always rejected the supernatural, always drawn to the more rational explanation for things. But now, after everything that had transpired and her newfound abilities, Nick knew he had to be careful with her. He couldn't just unleash the full weight of his experiences upon her fragile psyche.

And so, Nick recounted the tale of Leo's influence, Quinn's betrayal, and the unraveling of dark secrets that had haunted their town for years. He spoke of the spirits he had encountered and the supernatural powers that had awakened within him. His family listened intently, their eyes wide with wonder and disbelief. They asked questions, seeking to understand the depths of Nick's experiences, and he answered as best he could, grateful for their open minds and unwavering support.

Nick sighed, reaching out to hold Missy's hand gently. "I know it's hard for you. Trust me, I understand. But seeing ghosts is just the beginning. There's so much more to this world than meets the eye, and I know I've only scratched the surface."

Missy frowned, her brow furrowing in concern. "I want to understand, Nick. I want to be a part of this. Well, I guess I *am* part of it. I really have no choice, do I? But you, Nick, what if it's dangerous? What if you get hurt? I don't want anything bad to happen to you. You could have died in the square."

He didn't tell them that he actually did die — for two long minutes.

His father nodded in agreement. "That's true, son. We were all worried. But always remember you're never alone. Your mother and I are here for the both of you, every step of the way. We'll support you in whatever you choose to do."

His mother chimed in, her voice filled with determination. "Yes, Nick. You have a gift, and it's up to you how you use it." She turned to Missy. "And the same goes for you, Missy. All I can ask the both of you is to remember to always follow your heart and make choices that align with your values."

Gabe, who had been sitting quietly on the other end of the couch taking it all in, looked at Nick with a newfound respect in his eyes. Gabe had been there for him through it all, from the moment they first encountered Leo to the heart-stopping climax in the square. He had witnessed

Nick's transformation firsthand, and it had only deepened their bond.

Later that evening, as the house settled into a comforting silence, Nick stood outside his bedroom door, which was now Gabe's bedroom. Nick had agreed to move to the basement while Gabe stayed with them. He hesitated outside the door for a moment, his heart pounding with a mix of anticipation and longing.

Nick gently pushed open the door, revealing a room that was bathed in the soft glow of twinkling fairy lights strung across the walls. It was a space that held countless memories — from childhood adventures to teenage secrets shared under the cover of darkness. But tonight, it seemed different.

Inside, Gabe sat on Nick's bed, his face illuminated by the warm light of a bedside lamp. He looked up as Nick entered, and their eyes met — an unspoken understanding passing between them. Without a word, they moved towards each other and embraced, their bodies melting together as if they were two halves of a whole. The tension of the day slipped away as they held each other, finding comfort in the familiarity of their touch.

Nick buried his face in Gabe's chest, inhaling his intoxicating scent. As they stood there, wrapped in each other's arms, Nick was grateful for Gabe's unwavering support. Throughout their journey, Gabe had been his anchor — the steady presence that kept him grounded when everything else seemed to fall apart.

I couldn't have done any of this without you, you know," Nick whispered, his voice filled with emotion. "You've been with me every step of the way, and I'm so grateful for that."

Gabe leaned back slightly to look into Nick's eyes, his gaze filled with tenderness. "Nick, *you're* the one who has shown incredible strength and resilience. I've never met anyone like you, and I'm honored to be by your side, always. I caught me a good one!"

They shared a soft kiss, their lips meeting in a gentle caress. As they parted, Gabe took Nick's hand in his own and led him to the bed. They sat down together, their fingers intertwined. They spoke softly, finding joy, calm and familiarity in each other's presence.

EPILOGUE

NICK STOOD in the shadow of the looming Gallowspine Mountains, their jagged peaks cutting a stark silhouette against the twilight sky. He watched Missy, her brow furrowed in concentration as she traced symbols in the air, Katrina guiding her hand with an encouraging nod. The arcane gestures shimmered briefly before dissipating into the cool evening breeze.

"Like this?" Missy asked, her voice a mix of determination and fatigue.

"Exactly like that," Katrina replied, her tone soft but firm. "You have a natural affinity for the craft."

Nick couldn't help but smile at his sister's progress. He had spent countless days of his gap year passing down the knowledge that he had amassed. The secrets that once made him feel like an outcast were now a bond between them. Unlike their father, who had shied away from the family legacy, Missy embraced it wholeheartedly. She had refused to work with tarot cards, however — she said they gave her the creeps, and Nick respected that. Every medium had their own way with the spirits — or so says Katrina.

"Nick, are you okay with leaving her?" Gabe's voice cut through Nick's reverie, pulling his gaze away from Missy.

"Missy's got this," Nick said, clapping his friend on the shoulder. "Besides, she's in expert hands with Katrina." He shoved his hands into the pockets of his jacket, feeling the weight of change hanging in the air like the early autumn mist.

Gabe nodded, leaning against the rustic fence that bordered their property. "I still can't believe your folks took me in like I was one of their own," he said after a moment, his voice tinged with gratitude and lingering disbelief.

"Hey, you're family now," Nick replied, sincerity warming his words. "And Mom and Dad — they care about you, man. You know they do."

"Even if my own parents want nothing to do with me anymore."

"Money isn't love, Gabe." Nick frowned, thinking about the legally obligated monthly checks that arrived with mechanical precision from Gabe's estranged parents. It was their cold, calculated way of washing their hands of him.

"Guess not," Gabe murmured, kicking at a loose pebble on the ground.

Nick gazed back at Missy, who was now laughing at something Katrina said. His heart swelled with pride, and he felt a pang of protectiveness. He knew he was leaving her in capable hands, but the thought of being miles away unsettled him more than he cared to admit.

"Ready for this new chapter?" Gabe asked, breaking into his thoughts.

"Ready as I'll ever be," Nick said, though uncertainty gnawed at him. He looked up at the mountains again. Nick shook his head slightly, trying to dispel the unease.

"Come on," Gabe said, pushing off from the fence. "Let's go say goodbye to your sister. Then we've got a long drive ahead of us tomorrow."

"Right behind you," Nick promised, his gaze lingering on Missy for a moment longer before he followed Gabe across the dew-kissed grass.

Later, Nick and Gabe stood at the edge of the overlook, where the world dropped away into a sea of shadowy pines. A chill breeze tousled Gabe's blond hair.

"Seems quieter now, doesn't it?" Gabe's voice broke through the silence as he joined Nick, his breath misting in the cooling air.

Nick nodded, his eyes scanning the horizon. "Yeah. The ghosts are few and far in between these days." As he spoke, a sense of accomplishment threaded through him. He had become adept at guiding lost souls to their rest, a reaper who found solace in giving peace to the departed.

"Missy's got a good handle on things," Gabe continued, resting a hand on Nick's shoulder. "You've taught her well."

"Thanks, man. And Dad's stepping up too," Nick replied, though he couldn't quite picture his father soothing the bereaved. Still, the idea that his family would keep the town safe in his absence was a comfort.

"Pre-med, huh? Duke's going to be intense," Nick said, changing the subject. He watched Gabe's face light up with a mix of pride and apprehension.

"Can you believe it? Never thought they'd accept me when I applied. But I'm ready for it. Ready to help people... in the daylight, for a change," Gabe said with a wry smile. "I'm just grateful that my parents didn't empty out the college fund account they'd set aside. Or maybe the forgot about the account?"

"I hope you transferred it somewhere else."

"Oh, hell yes," Gabe said. "Your father cosigned on a savings account for me the other day and we transferred all my college money over to the new one. Your dad also said he'd help out with a loan if I needed it."

"Like I've always told you, they're crazy about you."

"So, are you excited about your studies?"

Nick nodded. "Criminal justice, here I come! I think all my mystery solving and ghost hunting over the past couple of years will come in handy." Nick's joke was an attempt to lighten the mood, but deep down, he harbored a genuine desire to solve crimes, to bring closure, much like he did as a medium.

Gabe chuckled. "A doctor and a cop, sounds like the start of a poor joke."

"Or the beginning of something great," Nick mused, allowing himself a small smile. It was difficult to imagine that only a year ago, he had been knee-deep in supernatural troubles and had even died. Now, he was on the cusp of a new adventure — one rooted in the living world.

They both turned as a gust of wind stirred the leaves, a reminder of the mountain's enduring presence.

"Should we head back?" Gabe asked, glancing over his shoulder toward the path that led home.

"In a minute." Nick took a deep breath, his gaze fixed on the fading light. He could feel the pull of the unknown tugging at the edges of his mind.

The mountains had been his training ground, a place of trials and triumphs. As he prepared to leave them behind, he knew the skills he honed here would serve him well.

"Tomorrow's a big day," Gabe said softly, sensing the weight of the moment.

"So let's make tonight count," Nick affirmed, the finality of the statement echoing in his heart.

Together, they turned from the vista, their footsteps crunching on the gravel path as they made their way back to where family and farewells awaited. The mountains loomed behind them, a silent guardian watching over the paths they would each take come morning.

A FEW WEEKS LATER, Nick's fingers paused over the keyboard, the blue glow of his laptop casting an eerie light across his otherwise darkened dorm room. The clock on his desk read just past midnight, and the rest of Plymouth State University was quiet — save for the distant laugh of some night owl students enjoying their newfound freedom.

"Come on," he muttered to himself, clicking through another link as he dived back into the web of campus legends that had caught his attention. Every strand intertwined to form a complex web of ghost tales that enveloped Plymouth State like a ghostly veil.

"Still hunting ghosts, huh?" came a voice from the doorway. Gabe leaned against the frame, his own laptop bag slung over one shoulder. He'd made the drive up from Duke for the weekend, swapping his pristine lab coat for a worn leather jacket.

"Can't help it," Nick replied with a half-smirk, leaning back in his chair. He had left his room door open, anxiously awaiting Gabe's arrival. "It's like they're following me."

"Or you're drawn to them," Gabe countered, stepping into the room and dropping onto the edge of Nick's bed.

"Maybe." Nick shrugged, glancing back at the screen where another article loaded. "But look at this — Plymouth State University is rumored to be haunted. Seems I've got a set of local haunts right here to keep me busy," Nick said, scrolling through eyewitness accounts of cold spots and phantom footsteps.

"Should've figured," Gabe quipped, tossing his bag aside. "So what's the plan? Nighttime stakeouts between Criminal Justice classes?"

"Something like that," Nick mused, leaning forward as he clicked on a grainy image of a shadowy figure caught on a security camera. His finger hovered over the mouse pad, tracing the contours of the apparition. A chill ran down his spine, not from fear, but from the thrill of the chase.

Gabe's expression shifted between skepticism and intrigue."Seriously, man. Most people go to college to get away from the family business. You took it with you."

"Guess you can take the boy out of Gallowspine Mountains, but you can't take Gallowspine Mountains out of the boy," Nick said, his thoughts drifting back to the rugged peaks that had shaped him.

"Speaking of which," Gabe started, his tone shifting to something more serious, "you talk to Missy lately?"

"Yesterday," Nick answered, closing his laptop with a snap. "She's handling things well. Dad's even pitching in, which is... surreal."

The room fell silent for a moment, filled with the weight of everything left unsaid. They both knew the cost of embracing the shadows that lurked just beyond sight.

"New ghostly adventures ahead, then?" Gabe finally broke the silence, nodding toward the closed laptop.

"Without a doubt," Nick confirmed, rising from his seat. He crossed the room to flick on the lamp, chasing away the darkness with a soft, golden hue. "And you'll be patching up the living while I deal with the dead."

"Alright, Detective Reaper," Gabe said with mock formality. "Let's grab some late-night grub. Your treat."

"Deal," Nick agreed, grabbing his wallet and keys. "But we're avoiding the library. That's where most of the 'sightings' happen."

"Scared?" Gabe teased as they stepped out into the hallway.

"Cautious," Nick corrected, locking the door behind them. Their voices faded into the quiet as they walked down the corridor. Ahead of them, the night beckoned, vast and uncharted, whispering of new mysteries yet to be revealed.

THE END

PLEASE LEAVE A REVIEW

If you enjoyed this book and have a moment to spare, please consider leaving a short review wherever you purchased this book. They can be long, short, or in between. Even a star rating is great.

Your help in spreading the word is gratefully appreciated. Also consider telling your friends, family or even random strangers about it to help me spread the word about my book.

Thank you so much for supporting my work!

Questions? Comments? I'd love to hear from you! Contact me at: roger@rogerhyttinen.com

CONNECT WITH ME

Visit the link below for my newsletter, including exclusive stories, bonuses, and advance notice about upcoming work.

https://rogerhyttinen.com/newsletter

Connect with me:

Facebook:
https://www.facebook.com/rogerhyttinen.author

Visit My Blog:
https://rogerhyttinen.com

ROGER'S BOOKS

Standalones

A Touch of Cedar

Christmas Cookies that Sparkle

Pushed Under the Mistletoe

Ghost Oracle Series:

Nick's Awakening (Ghost Oracle Book 1)

Anaconda! (Ghost Oracle Book 2)

The Magician's Secret (Ghost Oracle Book 3)

Ghost at the Prom (Book 4)

Camping with A Ghost (Book 5)

Wolves of Norbury series:

Norian's Gamble

STAY IN THE KNOW

Want to know be the first to know when I release a new book?

Then join my newsletter.

Be the first to know when I'm about to release a new novel, share a cover release, or offer freebies and other goodies (like a free short story in your inbox every Monday!).

To sign up for my newsletter, visit my site at: https://roger-hyttinen.com/newsletter